Evil Was a Child Once

Wendra Colleen

Published by Wendra Colleen, 2024.

EVIL WAS A CHILD ONCE

First edition. October 1, 2024.

Copyright © 2024 Wendra Colleen.

ISBN: 979-8990986817

Written by Wendra Colleen.

Also by Wendra Colleen

Facades of Life and Death
Hello Darkness
Sins of Our Fathers
The Dark Light Of His Gift
The Lost Girl
The Ravenous
Evil Was a Child Once

Watch for more at https://www.wendracolleen.com.

Table of Contents

CHAPTER 1—EVIL

B *oston, Massachusetts—Summer*
Twelve-year-old Evil Mather sat at the long dining room table, two large red candles on either side of her, the flames wavering. She sucked in ragged breaths, her face stained with tears. With her wrists bound together in her lap, she lifted them and took a final swipe at her eyes, pushing away thick red curls from her face. The silk didn't hurt, but the double knots ensured their strength. Her father, Reverend Stanley Mather, stood behind her and patted her shoulders. The Reverend moved to stand in front of her, his long grayish hair brushing his shoulders and the silver Mather family crest around his neck winking in the candlelight, bright against the black robes.

"I'm so sorry, Evil." His deep voice filled the room, a bow drawn across the lowest cello strings. "I think it's horrible what that girl did, and I don't blame you for being angry, not at all. You know your name is not your fault. But remember that we can harness your emotion during these times to find the diary."

"These things wouldn't happen if I were normal, right, Father?" Evil sniffled. "If I could get rid of the Curse?"

"That's right," her father assured her. "Find the diary, cure the Curse."

"Find the witches, find the diary," she automatically responded in a shaky voice.

"But? No matter what?"

"I mustn't draw Father, I mustn't draw myself." She swallowed. "But what if...what if I hadn't come to you just now...?"

The Reverend pulled up a dining chair to sit beside her, taking her chilled bound hands into his. "You know what would happen. And that's why I'll always be here for you. You can only trust me to guide your drawings, not yourself. We can't change the past, Evil, but we can shape the future."

He squeezed her hands and smiled. "And all those drawings are in the past. What you did to those children was an accident." He pointed to the silk knots. "And this is how we shape the future." He inhaled deeply. "Do you think you can channel your feelings so we can find the diary?"

She swallowed again, then nodded. *Maybe...maybe this time I won't hurt anyone.* But she didn't believe it. Someone always got hurt when she drew, even if her father reassured her that drawing was "absolutely necessary."

He pulled a large sketch pad and several pencils from the dark end of the table and placed them before Evil. The Reverend's hands hovered over the silk knots at her wrists.

"You give me your word you will not draw the girl who hurt your feelings? You will only think of the witches as I speak to you?"

Evil silently nodded again, then whispered, "I don't want to hurt anybody. I just want to be normal."

The Reverend clasped her bound hands in his, his eyes shining. "I know. And I feel certain that your drawings will tell us where the witches are hiding the diary. Once we have it, I know it will tell us how to defeat the Curse."

Her father's fingers tugged and unwound the silken knots, and Evil exhaled. She rolled her wrists, flexing her fingers. She grasped a pencil in each hand, and her father began to speak as he rested his hands on her shoulders once more. He told a story—like always—that ended with a question. And then she would draw the answer. Evil never knew what the answer would look like on the page, and she often didn't know what it meant when she was done. But something always happened. Something bad.

"For twelve years, a girl has tried to be good. Her father loves her dearly. Nothing pains him more than when she comes home with a broken heart again and again. Children mock her name. A name she must bear solely because of a Curse. She is a good girl, but what she draws hurts others. She is a good girl, but she has no friends. She is a *good* girl, but her life was cursed hundreds of years ago by the very people who harbor her cure, her great-great-great-grandfather's diary. Doesn't a girl whose heart is good deserve to be cured?"

As her father spoke, Evil's heart pounded, and tears pricked at her eyes again. This was not just any story—it was her story. Her father continued.

"Where can we find these descendants of the witches? Where did they flee so long ago?"

Gradually, her heart slowed. Evil's eyes fluttered, drooped, and finally closed. She sensed her hands starting to move across the page, slowly at first, then faster. And faster. Then everything went black like always.

Evil burst into consciousness again, gasping as her eyes flew open and the darkness receded. She knew the drawing must be complete. The paper slid out from under her hands as her vision sharpened. She bit her lip and twisted her neck slightly to watch her father's face as he gazed at the paper.

His brow wrinkled and his eyes narrowed as he scanned the drawing. Evil held her breath. Then his expression cleared and the corners of his mouth slowly turned up. He lowered the drawing and looked at her.

"It's not frightening, I promise. And you know we can't burn these because we want them to happen, so you will have to see it sooner or later."

Evil swallowed, shuddering at the memories of scrawling in hurt and anger after so much bullying at school. She nodded for him to turn it around. He flipped the page toward her, and she braced herself despite what her father had said about it not being frightening.

The sketch of an open journal spread out before her, the writing so full of swoops and swirls that Evil couldn't read it.

"Does it mean anything to you, Evil? Can you read the handwriting?"

Evil shook her head, then stopped. She leaned in, squinted.

"Father, I can read something. At the very top, there's some words that are spelled funny, but then there's something else printed above it."

Her father whipped the page back around to him, his eyes wide and eager like when she'd spied on him preaching.

"I was too hasty," he said, his voice light with excitement. He inspected the page. "Ah yes, there it is. The funny words are Latin, but it's what's printed above that matters."

"It's a place, isn't it, Father? Isn't it?" Evil clenched her hands to control her trembling.

"Yes. I believe we have a destination." The Reverend lowered the drawing, sweat beading on his forehead. "It says The Library of Strange and Unusual Things."

CHAPTER 2—DAVEY

96 days since the accident

Virtue, California—Fall

Ever since the accident, as he called it in his head, Davey Ellington only left his room for three reasons: to attend school, to run errands for his mother, and today, to visit The Library of Strange and Unusual Things.

He'd looked forward to sixth grade for a long time, but that had changed. It was nearing Halloween, and most days, especially at school, still reminded Davey of living underwater. Talking sounded gurgled, and his arms and legs moved slow and heavy. He came up for air at recess, sitting alone on a green bench at the edge of the playground. Sometimes he didn't know the bell had rung until a teacher shook him by the shoulder. In class, Davey stared at the clock above the teacher's desk, wondering when he could get back to his bedroom.

At home, Davey sat on the floor with his knees scrunched up between the wall and his bed. He imagined hearing his dad open the front door, imagined his gun belt clinking as he hung it on the coatrack. Then the soft sound of wood sliding across the carpet as he opened Davey's door. He'd stand at the side of the bed, in his police uniform, just like in the framed picture on Davey's nightstand. Davey had learned he could picture his dad near him if he tried not to look directly at him. Otherwise, he'd go away. It had to be enough to imagine the give of the bed as his dad sat down, too big to fit in the narrow space with Davey. He recalled the smell of his dad's aftershave mixed with a little sweat, like it had been a tough night.

The memory of the accident always interrupted at some point: the siren, the colored lights against the apartment building. Hushed voices speaking about his dad checking on a Dr. Hathorne because he hadn't been at work at the Library for days. No one knew Dr. Hathorne slept with a loaded gun. Dr. Hathorne, a stranger who ruined Davey's life forever. Then the same question running on an endless loop in his head: *Dad, why did you have to die?*

Davey couldn't even be angry with Dr. Hathorne because he'd died too. Heart attack. They found him in bed, his hand still wrapped around the gun that had killed his dad in the doorway, just a few feet away.

Everyone said the old man was crazy, he'd gone off of his medication, didn't know he was shooting a policeman. But why had he gone off his medication? Why had he gone crazy?

His dad had gone there to help. Why did he have to die?

Davey pulled on a jacket as he left the apartment around noon that Saturday in October. Davey and his parents used to go to the Library every Saturday at that time, but this would be his first visit since the accident. He missed it, but his ma said she couldn't go yet: "Oh no, you go, Davey, I have to make this casserole," and "I also have to check in at work because this one patient is not doing well at all..."

Because they'd been going there forever and his ma knew some of the staff, she let him go by himself. Besides, he'd been walking the whole town since he could remember. Virtue was the smallest and oldest town in California. And if he got confused, he just had to find the mansion on the hill. If he headed toward that, it would bring him back to his apartment. Of course, it was way up in the hills behind them, and he didn't even know if anyone lived there. When it was foggy like today, it looked like a mansion in the clouds.

Supposedly the Library was the oldest building in town. Davey assumed that's why it had this weird Latin phrase all over the place: *Evolutionis Doctrina*. He wasn't sure what it meant, but the writing looked cool. A much smaller version of the Library had been there in some form or another since Virtue was founded some two hundred years ago. Now it was much larger and had become a huge tourist attraction since they had acquired such neat stuff (gadgets, pictures, furniture, clothes, you name it). People had been making or donating things forever, and there hadn't always been a good system for tracking everything. You never knew what you were going to find beyond a column or a book, behind a lamp or a table. Plus, the tourist draw was how it came to be open twenty-four hours. Davey had never been there super late, but he liked the idea that when he was old enough, he could stay there until it was really dark.

"People think the Library just has books," Davey's dad would often prompt when the clock tower came into view. Together, he and his dad would shout, "Boy are THEY WRONG!" Being allowed to shout used to make Davey giggly.

Once his family entered the Library, they always went their separate ways: Ma to Southern History or Cooking or Literature, Dad to WWII or Science Fiction, and Davey to the Children's Realm. And if anyone thought Davey went there solely to read...

Boy were they wrong.

Davey often lost himself in the Library's *stuff* as much as its books.

In the Children's Realm, a path like the yellow brick road wound its way throughout the stacks. It looked real until you stepped on it—actually soft, shiny plastic. A few girls always stood around Cinderella's dress with its big skirt and puffy sleeves, the fabric all shimmery underneath a glass dome. A light kept switching colors so the gown sparkled yellow, then blue, then silver, and back again.

Davey loved the display from *Charlie and the Chocolate Factory*: A row of WONKA chocolate bars sat on a wooden shelf, but the bar in the middle had the wrapper pulled back just enough to see the top part of a golden ticket.

Once a year, the Library staff hid what they called the latest *children's acquisition* somewhere in the Realm. They announced the book that inspired the object months ahead and had several copies on hand to make sure everyone could read it. They called it *The Realm Treasure Hunt,* and the clues were all connected to that year's book. Over a year ago, at the beginning of fifth grade, Davey had found the hidden object, which turned out to be a thick length of rope with vines around it—the rope the kids used to cross into Terabithia from *Bridge to Terabithia.*

Davey's prize came in the form of a small scroll, the paper wrinkled and brown like it was old. It even had a real wax seal, a pattern of circles in a triangle. Davey was told it could only be opened by Library staff, but it could be exchanged for a private tour of the towers where the public wasn't allowed to go. He and his dad had been planning to do the tour together when his schedule permitted, but then the accident had happened. Davey kept the scroll in the front pocket of his backpack, hoping he would want to take the tour someday.

Sometimes, though, like today, Davey wanted to search for something whether a Hunt was on or not. The feeling tugged at him as the clock tower came into view, a floating ring of mist hovering around its neck. *Little Ben,* his dad used to call it, saying it reminded him of a much larger clock in London. As Davey made his way across the vast stretch of grass, he craned his neck to take in all thirteen stories of the Library. Davey counted the four spires as the thirteenth floor, even if the public wasn't allowed in them. Davey had been surprised the first time he heard visitors exclaiming, "*This* is a library?" and "This place is more like a haunted castle than a library!" He wondered what other libraries looked like because this one, with worn stones as big as him, towers at all four corners, and so many rooms it was like a maze, was the only one Davey had ever known.

The Library loomed above the main entrance, thirty-five stone steps, wide enough that several buses full of kids could clamber up them with space to spare. Two monsters called *gargoyles* guarded either side of the steps. Davey had stopped cold when he first saw them as a little kid, the larger-than-life stone creatures with their fangs and long shadows. While they had bodies somewhat like giant dogs, their heads resembled nothing Davey could understand—like some mashed-up combination of a lion and a person with big eyes and sharp teeth. His ma and dad had taken a few steps, then turned back to him.

"Come on, son," his dad called, gesturing up the steps.

Davey, mute with fear, pointed to the monsters and shook his head. The monsters clearly didn't want him to pass.

His dad looked at his ma, and each took one of Davey's hands. While his dad's pale hands made Davey's seem quite brown, they faded next to his ma's darker hands. His ma bent down and stage-whispered in his ear.

"Now, Davey, your dad has been looking forward to you counting these steps. He knows you are the best counter in Virtue. You're not going to let him down, are you?"

Davey snuck a peek at his dad, who quickly gazed up at the stone steps and sighed. "It's okay, Davey, I guess...I guess we'll never know how many there are." His dad paused. "Shame that all the toys are up these stairs too. But we'll have fun just walking around the grounds, right?"

And that's how Davey learned there were thirty-five steps.

Most first-time visitors and tourists took the steps because they were *stately* and *grand*. But for Davey, he never got tired of counting them, even in his head.

Davey put a foot on the bottom step as children raced past him, adults shouting at their backs. Young and old tourists snapped pictures of the gargoyles. But Davey looked at his shoe on the stone step.

One...

Before long, he'd reached the top, inhaling deeply. The sun blinded him a little as it glared off the cool marbled terrace. He gradually caught his breath and then entered what he called the Time Tunnel, though the large sign announced it as the Hall of Murals.

"Ready, Davey?" his dad had asked the first time he took Davey there, grinning as he took his son's hand, and the three of them stepped into the large, cool Time Tunnel.

Through a combination of paint and tiny lights embedded in the ground, the Tunnel led into dawn, surrounded by pink and orange light and soft, fluffy clouds. Davey had turned around to make sure the real world was still behind him. As he walked into dawn, the clouds peeled away around him, and the sun rose over his head. It burned so brightly against the blue sky it hurt his eyes.

Advancing through the Tunnel, the sun moved and gradually dipped, the blue sky darkening. And just before reaching the large double glass doors to enter the Library, a velvety night splashed with stars wrapped everyone who entered in a dark, still blanket. Despite the lights shining down from the ceiling, the black walls on the main floor continued with millions (billions?) of stars. It quieted people like they were in church.

As Davey stepped inside, alone, the memories of his parents beside him vanishing, he smelled the familiar scents of cedar and lemons, the staff ever polishing the staircase and endless bookcases. The main floor had a large staff area with desks behind a wooden counter that almost came up to Davey's chin. Hallways fingered off the left side of the circulation desk and general staff area, each ending in doors to inner stairways. On the other side of the room sat a gigantic, twisting staircase that led up to the most popular floors. Davey usually went straight to the Children's Realm. Most of the Library was still a mystery. He liked that.

But now the urge to search for something made him want to explore, so Davey turned left and chose the first hallway, heading for the door at the end. Unlike at his more modern school, all the doors here were made of dark wood and stood a good foot taller like the front entrances of rich houses. Even the handles were different from school—instead of the silver knobs, these had iron handles that pushed down.

At the end of the first hallway, he thought the door was locked, but as he pressed down harder, the handle clicked, and he pushed it open. He cocked his head to one side because these stairs going up looked like a much smaller version of the stone steps outside. The light seemed different too—and then Davey spied a fake candle sitting in a space carved into the wall.

"Cool," Davey said to himself as he touched the clear plastic flame. Davey picked it up from the black base and inspected the bottom.

Batteries. Thought so.

He made his way up the stairs, his sneakers making loud scraping sounds against the bare stone. He passed landings that led to locked rooms with carved metal labels (*The Plath Room*, *The Woolf Room*—funny because they spelled *wolf* wrong—*The Shelley Room*).

He decided he would take a break at the next landing no matter what.

At the next landing, strips of black, filmy material like the kind made from fancy lady scarves hung over a large entrance the size of a wall. The fabric rippled and shimmered, and letters made of light rose and fell as the strips billowed.

Davey read the big block letters as the strips came together, and his throat dried on the spot.

THE LAND OF SCIENCE FICTION. Dad's territory.

For a moment he didn't move, but then his hand parted the waving cloth and he stepped through. He hadn't been there since the accident. He hadn't realized he'd been avoiding it.

Davey looked up at the domed ceiling, a dusky orangey-red that his dad said was supposed to remind people of Mars. To fit the round room, all the bookshelves arced and curved away from the center like waves in a pool. Long open paths that gradually narrowed sliced through the shelves and allowed people to walk in and around the stacks.

He walked until he found *Dune*. He touched the yellow spine, wondering if anyone else had touched it since his dad last held it. He replaced it and moved closer to the center. Davey stood on his tiptoes and pulled down *Childhood's End*.

Would he know if his dad had held it? Would he be able to tell?

He spied a small black devil figurine behind this book, bat-like wings spread out behind him. It almost made him smile. He carefully slid the book back in place.

Davey continued farther into the room until he came to a tall, narrow arch of a bookshelf. It held all the books of one author.

Ray Bradbury. His dad's all-time favorite.

Davey ran his hands over the spines. His dad said that if you pulled on the right Ray Bradbury book, a secret passageway would open and transform the Library into Mars.

Davey's heart sped up. If his dad were anywhere, it would be there. In Bradbury's Mars, full of swirling sand and golden-eyed Martians like in *The Martian Chronicles*.

He scrounged a footstool and then began at the top, pulling out a book, waiting, putting it back. Then he started closing his eyes as he did it.

Dad, tell me which book it is. Please tell me.

After pulling out so many books, he reached the last book on the bottom shelf: a laminated, signed copy of *Something Wicked This Way*

Comes. He pulled it out and held it to his chest. He tried to imagine what Mars smelled like, sounded like. He didn't want to open his eyes.

Please. Please. Dad, tell me where you are.

"I love that book," a voice whispered.

Davey gasped; his eyes flew open and he looked to his right.

There stood a girl with long, flaming red hair, skin as pale as bone.

The book slipped from his hands.

The girl caught the book in her ghostly hands before it hit the floor. She held it to her chest and took a step back, casting a wary glance at Davey.

Davey froze, speechless. Unlike the girls at school, she had wild hair, so dark red it seemed purple in places and spilling out all over the place like it had fought a hairbrush and won. She also wore a man's white shirt, the kind his dad used to wear, buckled at the waist with a man-sized belt. Her pants hung far above her ankles as if they'd shrunk. She was like something out of a circus.

She blinked rapidly. "It's about a carnival, not a circus," she said in a loud whisper, tapping *Something Wicked This Way Comes* with her fingers. She gazed around. "How did I miss this floor?"

Wait, had he said what he was thinking out loud? About the circus?

She held the book out to him, but Davey didn't move. She bent down again and slid the book back into place, so close to his ankles he jumped off the footstool. She startled, too.

"Sorry," she mumbled. Then she looked up at him.

He caught his breath because he'd never seen eyes like that before. Gray? Blue? Some combination? Her eyes grew bigger as she stared back at Davey.

"I'm sorry," she repeated, this time with a catch in her voice, "for what happened to you."

She turned and her curls flew behind her as she disappeared into the maze of bookshelves. Davey wasn't sure how long he stood there after that.

CHAPTER 3—DAVEY

97 days since the accident

On Sunday, Davey headed toward the Library once more. He couldn't stop thinking about that girl he'd seen. Was she part of some event, with her weird clothes? Sometimes the Library held skits to promote a new collection or special object.

His ma expressed surprise and then relief that he wanted to leave the apartment again. He tried to remember when he last left on a Sunday and couldn't. He didn't count the Sundays before the accident.

"You want me to go with you, honey?" she asked.

His ma's face showed fear, but he honestly said no, that it was okay for him to go alone.

When he arrived on the main floor of the Library, a small crowd stood around a large, fancy painted sign. Davey stood on tiptoe but couldn't see what the sign said. Instead, he listened to what people were saying.

"No one knows who sent the diary; they found an anonymous letter in Dr. Hathorne's pocket."

"I don't know if I even want to go. I heard the Mather diary is cursed."

"Oh, please, Dr. Hathorne was ancient; the diary had nothing to do with his death."

"Oh, really? What about all his notes in his journal? Sounds like he was obsessed with it!"

At the mention of Dr. Hathorne, Davey's heartbeat filled his ears. Why were they talking about him? Part of him wanted to ask, but another part of him wanted to run. He stuffed his hands in his pockets and turned on his heel.

He half ran across the main floor to the hall to find the stone stairwell, but this time a sign stood in front of it: Closed for Maintenance. Davey grimaced but reasoned that many other stairwells needed exploring. And there were several entrances to the various floors, he'd heard. Maybe the girl was somewhere else today.

He stood still in front of the Closed for Maintenance sign. Why *would* she be here again?

He shifted from one foot to the other. Why did he care?

Davey turned and walked back out of the hall. As he stood wondering which stairway to take next, a familiar poster taped to a column caught his eye, its bright blue, red, and green swirls making his heart thump with excitement out of habit:

The Realm Treasure Hunt: Will You Be the Next Winner?

Davey relaxed. That's why he wanted to find her. It was just another hunt. Something he loved...or...used to love. He turned away from the poster and went down the next hallway.

But this stairwell was closed for a special event.

Davey wrinkled his nose in confusion at all the signs. He reached out and tried the handle anyway, but it didn't give. He shrugged, moving on to the last hall.

Another sign. Private: Do Not Enter.

Davey threw up his hands in frustration and stomped in a circle. He exhaled sharply and pressed his lips together.

His hand closed over the handle. Pushed down. *Click.*

He sucked in his breath. Because now he knew he would be doing something wrong if he entered, which the sign clearly said not to. Ma taught him to follow the rules. And what would the Library staff do if they caught him?

Davey turned to leave, but his heart sank. He turned back.

But what if I just look? Then I'm not entering.

Davey stole a glance behind him to make sure the hall was empty. People passed at the very end, eyes forward or buried in a book as they strolled.

Davey braced himself against the frame so his feet stayed out of the forbidden hall. He quietly pushed the door open, just enough for him to stick his head in.

He blinked in the grainy darkness. As his eyes adjusted, he could make out a dank hall with an earthy smell that reminded him of the stone stairwell from yesterday. A light shone at the end of the hall from a tall, curved entryway.

Someone passed in front of it. It was fast, but it looked like someone with red hair.

His ma's rules tumbled from his mind. He walked quickly into the hall, a chill settling around his shoulders. When he came to the archway, though, thick red carpet covered the floor, and he hesitated to step on it, swiveling his head left and right for the girl.

He didn't see anyone, just a long dining table with silky place mats at either end that matched the carpet. Davey looked up. A glass chandelier hung over the table, giving the room its soft light. Davey resisted the urge to count all the glass droplets or guess the weight of something so big.

Past the table, into another hall, a door faced him. Davey placed a sneakered toe on the carpet and whipped it back, but nothing happened. He planted a full foot. Still nothing.

Davey swallowed as he skittered across the short distance, thinking of the game he used to play when he had friends, pretending the floor was lava as they scrambled to stay on furniture. He easily reached the door, which, to his relief, was ajar. He didn't touch it, which somehow felt worse than just nosing his way in, and so he used his nose to nudge it enough so he could see.

Inside, penciled drawings on large pieces of paper covered everything: a small cot, a nightstand, the floor, the walls, even the ceiling. Davey's stomach clenched. The pictures weren't normal somehow. Many had parts of faces and close-ups of big eyes, yelling mouths...disembodied hands held up against...what? These pictures showed a lot of fear. People were running toward or away from things, throwing up hands to protect themselves. Or falling.

Something grabbed his shoulder, and Davey yelped. *I'm sorry, Ma!*

Two large hands gripped his shoulders and turned him. Davey looked up at a man with long, silvery hair and gray eyes.

Davey closed his eyes and whimpered. Then his nose twitched. The smell of wood smoke rose from the man's clothes.

"Father, no!" squeaked a girl's voice, and Davey opened his eyes as the pressure left his shoulders. The girl stood between them.

Over a mass of red curls, he saw the man straightening and backing up. He held up his hands. Shiny black robes dusted the floor, and his sleeves billowed at the ends.

"Evil, don't get excited. I found an intruder, and I'm taking care of it."

Davey's heart pounded with a mixture of fear and shame, but then he struggled to understand everything the man had said.

Why had the scary man said "evil" just now?

"No, he's not intruding! He's my...friend." She still shielded Davey.

The man grew calm and clasped his hands in front of him. "Friend?" He said the word like he didn't know what it meant. The girl's head lowered.

"I mean, I know him. From the Library."

The man folded his arms, something silver gleaming at his neck. Davey squinted. A bunch of circles and triangles?

"You don't want to risk upsetting anything, do you?"

The fiery hair swished back and forth in front of Davey's face.

"Then you'll show this young man out?"

The curls bounced up and down.

"And? Since you're upset?"

"I mustn't draw Father, I mustn't draw myself," she chanted.

Davey inhaled. He couldn't smell smoke anymore. Had he imagined it?

The man pointed his arm toward the hall entrance. She grabbed Davey's hand and walked swiftly to the hall.

"He didn't mean to... I mean, he's just trying to protect me," she stammered once they stood in the hall.

"No, I'm, uh, sorry, but...th-that's...your dad?" Davey managed to get out.

"He's just looking out for me," she said, nodding with a grave expression. They reached the door back to the Library. "He doesn't want anything to go wrong. We've waited forever." She pulled the door the rest of the way open and stood to the side so Davey could go back through.

Davey shook his head, trying to clear his thoughts. "Waited for what?"

Her eyes darted back to the room. She leaned toward him and whispered, "The diary! Somebody sent it here, but it belongs to Father."

The diary? He remembered the small crowd of people, and his insides twisted again. "You mean the one people are talking about out there?"

Her eyes lit up. "Are they?" she asked and stood on tiptoe as if she could see the crowd over Davey's head. "I guess that makes sense. Father is very important." Her gaze flickered again to the room as she spoke. "I should go." She tried to close the door behind Davey, but he held on to it.

"But what do you and your dad have to do with this diary thing? I don't understand. And what's back there?" He gestured with his free hand to the room behind them.

She swallowed and glanced away like she wanted to run, but then she leaned toward him again. "We live back there. The diary belongs to him, as the last living descendant of the Mathers. It's only on loan until it's restored."

Davey's jaw dropped. "You live here? At the Library?"

She nodded. "It's just a house that got bigger. And he insisted we live here so he could be close to the diary."

The man's voice boomed down the hall. "Evil!"

The girl's face grew panicked.

Something clicked for Davey.

"Why does he call you that?" he whispered.

She muttered a hasty apology as she gently shoved Davey the remainder of the way out of the hall. Davey heard the door lock this time.

What just happened? Davey stared at the wooden door, then looked back into the Library. He half wondered if he opened it again, would there still be a stone hallway? Would this girl and her dad still be there?

And why had the serious man—her *dad*—called her *evil*?

Davey retreated to the Children's Realm and picked up books he'd read many times. He found a corner with an overstuffed chair and curled up in it. He tried to lose himself in Dr. Seuss and *The Church Mouse,* tried to burrow into his childhood memories. But it didn't work today. He kept seeing the stern face of the silver-haired man, and questions swirled in his head.

That couldn't be her dad! A dad would never act like that.

His dad would never act like that.

And what was so darn important about this old diary? Why was everyone making such a big deal out of it? And if the diary had anything to do with Dr. Hathorne...

He shook his head, trying to erase that name.

Those sketches in that strange room... He had the sensation of tiny spiders crawling up his back just remembering them. To say the pictures were weird wasn't enough. What *were* they?

Instead of the books calming him, Davey read the same Dr. Seuss lines from *Oh, the Places You'll Go!* over and over. Not relaxing. Remembering. And not about his dad like he usually did but about the girl. Most of all, what she had said to him yesterday.

I'm sorry for what's happened to you.

What did she mean? What did she know?

It wasn't until that night, when he was in bed, that he realized when he talked with the girl, he could hear her just fine. Like they were both on land and not underwater.

CHAPTER 4—EVIL

7 days until the Anniversary

In their temporary living quarters in the Library, her father stood with his cold but comforting hands on her shoulders as Evil sat at the dining table. Her hands, each clutching a pencil, hovered over her sketch pad. Just like back home.

"You've done quite well so far, Evil." When she drew for him, her father's voice took on a smooth, chocolatey tone. "But today challenged you, didn't it?"

"I mustn't draw Father, I mustn't draw myself," Evil recited.

He sighed. "I wish I could say your trials were over, but you know this Anniversary will be the hardest challenge you face. I know you never liked staying in your room, but this will be far more difficult: the urge to draw could become even stronger, occur more frequently, and, most of all, the outcomes could be more violent than before. The Curse is not likely to give up without a fight."

She twisted around to gaze up at her father and couldn't resist repeating what she'd asked many times. "But why can't we prepare? Isn't there something we should be doing? You said this is my one chance!"

The Reverend squeezed her shoulder. "I'm doing all the preparing, you know that. Every day. All will fall into place."

"What will happen that day? How will I know what to do?"

"All will fall into place," her father repeated, and she knew that meant no more questions.

The Anniversary. Evil pursed her lips and tightened her hands around the pencils. How could her whole life come down to a single day?

Normally the October 30th Anniversary involved the dwindling members of the Mather Clan coming to Boston and celebrating the day that set the Clan on the path to a higher purpose: fighting the wicked. A witch might have cursed Cotton Mather in July, but on October 30th, he experienced "divine inspiration" concerning how to defeat it. So, that's the day the Clan celebrated. Her father always kept Evil in her room when the men arrived, though one time when she was very young, she snuck out and ran into one of the Mathers. The man froze at the sight of her, muttered "thief," crossed himself, then walked in the opposite direction. Her father found out and made her go to bed without dinner, but when Evil tearfully begged to know why the man thought she was a thief, her father hesitated and then said, "It's not your fault, Evil. It's just...the way things are."

"But why does he hate me?"

He refused to talk about it again.

Over time, though, she grew to look forward to the house filled with people, even if it was just men and she could only watch from a crack in her door. They laughed and swapped stories about "getting witches," and the house seemed strangely happy for a change.

This year, the Anniversary was a day of reckoning according to her father. A day so important that the Reverend said it would help him to lift the Curse. While previously Mathers came from all around to celebrate this holy day, this Anniversary would be just Evil and her father. The Reverend couldn't easily invite relatives when he had no place to put them, and more importantly, this Anniversary was for Evil most of all. Instead of hiding in her room while the Mathers celebrated, this time she would be the center of the celebration. "A new beginning," her father liked to say. With the diary, the Anniversary now meant the end of the Witch's Curse—for Evil and, her father believed, for the Clan as well.

When the Curse was lifted, Evil could be normal. She wouldn't hurt anyone with her drawings anymore. She might not even want to draw. And as for the Clan, the Mathers wouldn't get sick or hurt so often. So many had fallen off of high places, tripped into the paths of oncoming cars or trains, even accidentally electrocuted themselves since Evil was born. When someone had an accident, her father would say, "Blame the witches, blame the Curse." But he could stop saying that once he had read the diary and understood how to cure Evil once and for all.

She and her father only had to wait for the special Library *antiquarian* (which always made Evil think the person must look like a fish) to restore the diary. Then they—or rather her father—would be allowed to read it. And then he would know how to get rid of the Curse.

"We cannot be too careful," he said now, sitting at the dining table, two lit red candles on either side of Evil. "You cannot trust anyone but me. You cannot trust yourself. You trust *me*. All will fall into place on the Anniversary."

Her lower lip trembled.

"I know it's hard, but after the Curse is behind us, then you will have all the time in the world to make friends. Then you will have nothing to fear."

Evil took a shaky breath.

"He saw your room, Evil."

"But he wouldn't...!" she protested.

"But he could," her father interjected quietly. "Now," his tone deepened, "to the work at hand."

Evil sat up straighter and quieted. She closed her eyes.

"Think of the staff that you met today. Lawrence will be conducting minor, external repairs to the diary. We cannot have Lawrence reading the diary. Repairing it, yes, but only a Mather can *read* it." He paused. "You remember Lawrence, yes?"

Evil nodded.

Her father continued. "He lives on a meager salary, just enough to support himself and his wife. He is a loyal husband and is now the sole provider because his wife is quite ill. She can only dress and eat with his help right now, Evil. If he read the diary, something terrible would happen to him. She would be all alone, no one to care for her, no one to love her."

Evil swallowed and her hands shook.

"How do we keep him from reading the diary?" the Reverend asked.

Evil's breathing grew slower, deeper.

"This is critical, Evil. It's for our family. I wouldn't ask you to do this unless it was absolutely necessary."

Her father always said something like this when he asked her to draw for him.

"How do we keep Lawrence from reading the diary?" he rephrased.

Both of her hands moved across the page in different directions of their own accord. They moved faster, one hand sweeping across the page while the other made small, shading movements. Then Evil didn't know what her hands were doing because she drifted down into darkness like a dreamless sleep.

As her hands lifted off of the page, Evil opened her eyes. The candles looked the same as before she started, so she knew it had been quick.

Her father bent over her, peering at the drawing. "Very interesting. Let's hope he's not deterred from working on it altogether." He patted her shoulder. "After you're cured, I'll never ask you to draw again."

Evil bit her lip in worry as they both stared at the life-sized sketch of two wrinkled hands covered in angry, bubbling welts.

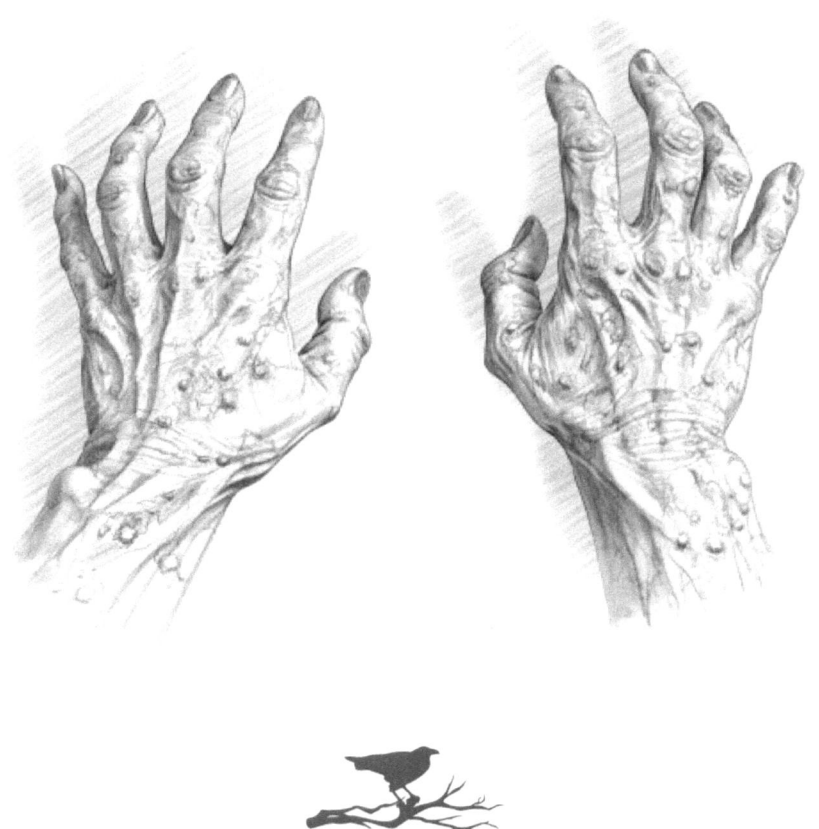

Evil lay on her cot, spent. Drawing left her tired like a run-down battery. She closed her eyes for a moment, imagining herself in her favorite chair in the Children's Realm.

For Evil, living at The Library of Strange and Unusual Things was the closest she'd ever come to directly experiencing happiness. Before, back in Boston, she had to go to school—even summer school—where teachers called her "Miss Mather" and the students made fun of her, ignored her, or worse, tormented her when no one was looking. She never knew what was going to be in her desk, in her lunch, on her seat.

No one tried to make her do anything at the Library. Her father expected her to make her own breakfast and lunch, and they shared dinner, like back home. He had one rule: *Don't leave the Library grounds.* And that was it. At first, Evil couldn't believe he wasn't going to snatch her freedom away. She stayed in bed for a long time, then crept around their living quarters. But each time her father walked in, he said, with a note of surprise, "Are you still here, Evil?" And then he would smile and head into his study.

It took over a week before Evil screwed up her courage to step into the Library all by herself, with no teachers, no students, no Father. The crowds of tourists both scared and excited her. But when she entered the Children's Realm and found the large, hardbound books with the soft, delicate drawings of fairies and queens, where girls with curses were cured and loved, her heart soared and laughter bubbled up from inside her.

I never want to laugh. Am I getting sick?

But the more she sat with the feeling, the lighter she felt, as if only the weight of the books kept her anchored to the ground. The more she told herself it was truly okay to explore, to read, to do what she wanted because her father said it was okay...the more she realized she liked this feeling.

Is this what...normal feels like?

By the end of the first week, Evil found a secluded chair where no one could see her in the Children's Realm. She cradled a giant fairy tale book and closed her eyes, just holding the book, holding the freedom. If she cherished the freedom, wrapped it up in gratitude, maybe it would want to stay.

Her eyelids fluttered, though, whisking her out of the comfort of the Children's Realm, filling her view instead with sketches of wide eyes and fear-stretched mouths, hands reaching out and closing on air, bodies falling from a great distance, skin shiny with sweat, and wild, sticky hair. Even though she'd created them, Evil shuddered. She really didn't know where these sketches came from because she never planned them at all, had no idea what she would see after her hands stopped moving.

Why does he call you Evil?

Her memory drifted back to Davey's question. She wanted to ponder it, turn it over like a rock. Her sleepy eyes slid over to a picture of a young boy running away from someone outside the scene, only a long shadow with hints of horns looming in his wake.

Oh. That's why. Unlike the boy in the picture—and many others—who had teased her about her name, Davey had seen her differently. He didn't say "Why are *you* called Evil?" but "Why does *he* call you Evil?" as if it might not be her real name. He didn't assume she was bad.

And I won't be bad for much longer.

The diary was the key; her father had figured that out. But how? How would it work? Her father only promised that it would have the answers. But he needed every day at the Library to "prepare." He said the diary would be hard to interpret, and he needed to conduct the proper research, but Evil overheard him in his study late at night on the phone and guessed a "list" also had something to do with the diary. She assumed he must be talking to the Clan members and was relieved they were willing to help, even if they weren't here.

When she had trouble sleeping in this new place, she overheard things like:

"*I have found one on the list. The actual descendant. Good.*"

And another time:

"*Not everyone on the list is going to be 'out' like she is, but I know they have to be here.*"

But the only thing she wanted from the diary was how to lift the Curse completely. Then she wouldn't be Evil anymore. Bad things would stop happening when she drew. She wouldn't *have* to draw when she got upset. She'd have friends.

Maybe she could be friends with that boy...if they stayed here for a while. But she and her father had never talked about after. It was always "when we find the diary..." What came after didn't matter. Because everything would be okay then.

Maybe, once she was free of the Curse...she could draw what she *wanted* to sketch, instead of giving in to the pressure in her chest that grew heavier and heavier...until she sketched it, let her feelings guide her fingers in ways she didn't understand. That urge, that pressure increased when her emotions rose up and grabbed her unexpectedly. And the feeling squeezed her tighter and tighter until she let her hands speak.

Once she was normal, maybe her father really would stop making...asking...her to draw people for him.

The pictures of faces with eyes squeezed shut in terror, bloody handprints, and swirling darkness blurred under her heavy lids. Her father made her keep the sketches up on the wall so he could *keep track of the redeemed*. That's what he called the people Evil drew, the ones he asked her to draw—the redeemed. He wrote the names and dates of those she'd drawn in a book. Evil didn't know how he could forget people he knew, especially his church members or their families. He saw them every Sunday back home. No one dared miss her father's sermons.

What were they doing on Sundays back in Boston with the Reverend gone? As Evil's eyes closed, she imagined the *parishioners*, as her father called them, filing into her father's church, the church that had been in the family for centuries. In her mind they arrived, orderly and silent, each of them taking a seat in the pews and training their attention on the pulpit. Her father didn't come, but they never moved and they never blinked.

As sleep pulled Evil down, the parishioners faded, and she slid into her recurrent dream. A dream where she was someone else.

She squinted, eyeing a figure in the distance.

The hunger that burned, the fear that swallowed her voice, and the chill that rattled her teeth all disappeared when she recognized him: the black coat, the jaunty way he rode the horse back and forth along the crowd. Like he thought someone might try to leave, turn away from the spectacle that was her. Or maybe he was just angling for the best view.

She straightened up, and the crowd around her hushed, leaned forward, eager. But when she gritted her teeth through the pain to extend her bony arm toward the man on the horse, the people in the crowd gawked, eyes wide, and the men and women in the crowd clutched at one another. Some crossed themselves. Her arm shook with the effort of pointing. She looked right at him. He didn't move on his horse anymore. She held him with her stare, her pointing finger, and then her croaking words.

It was all him, from the very beginning. And only she knew it.

But then something tightened around her neck and her heart quickened. She had to hurry, had to finish, they had to be—

Darkness.

Evil opened her eyes, gasping, her hands around her throat. She gulped air, grateful she'd left the light on in her room. She resisted staring at her arm as the sensation of pain faded like it always did. She took slow breaths until her pulse slowed too.

She waited to see if her fingers itched, meaning she'd have to draw, but she felt nothing. Thankfully. She didn't like having to turn drawings over to her father, to show him she couldn't control herself.

Would the dream also leave with the Curse?

She'd struggled to explain the dream to her father long ago. "An arm... I'm cold... I'm trying to say something...to the man on a horse." After confirming that she hadn't drawn anything, he'd only smiled and reassured her that dreams could not hurt her, that she had nothing to fear. Only the Curse was something to fear, and he would end it for her, once he had the diary.

She didn't tell him the dream repeated. And that over time, she remembered more details.

But what did the dream matter? It just kept repeating, and she hoped one day she'd understand why or that it would go away, along with the Curse.

Everything had to be okay once her father found the answers in her great-great-great-grandfather's diary, where it all started. And where, Evil had to believe, it would all end.

CHAPTER 5—DAVEY

98 days since the accident

Davey floated through school on Monday, rearranging the pieces of what happened at the Library like a puzzle. The teacher kept telling him when recess was, when lunch was. He was so in his head he forgot he was at school until someone called his name.

Davey wanted to tell his ma.

Ma, she lives in the part of the Library that used to be a house. She has this mean dad that calls her evil. They're here because of this old diary...

But the words wouldn't come. They sounded crazy enough in his head. And something nudged at him, something he didn't want to think about, warning him not to tell his ma. She already eyed him with that worried, funny look since the accident.

"Stick to the facts," his dad would say when Davey struggled to make sense of a problem. He'd probably start there, but what next? Davey shut one eye and cocked his head to the side, a habit when he thought hard.

His dad would know someone who knew about these people, someone who could give some details. Some nugget that would make Davey say, "Ooooh, I get it."

But his dad wasn't here. Davey's hollowed-out heart ached. *Why did you have to die...*

Suddenly he landed hard on the sidewalk, thrown backward, the wind knocked out of him. He swiveled his head left and right. When had school ended? A clock tower bonged nearby, and he blinked at the Library up ahead. When had he decided to walk to the Library?

An ice-blue eye leaned close, a thick shock of black hair covering the other eye like a pirate patch. And Johnny, a lanky sixth grader who towered over Davey, was about as nice as any pirate.

"Watch where you're going!" Johnny's breath smelled like sour milk. He'd moved here just before school started and immediately became the school's biggest bully. He had it in for Davey because he had to move here after the death of his grandfather, Dr. Hathorne. He chose to blame Davey for this, so Johnny became one more reminder of the accident. This made it easier for Davey to dislike Johnny rather than fear him, but in the end, Johnny was still the bigger kid.

Now Johnny lifted his head to gaze side to side, and Davey thought he knew why he was looking around: Johnny wanted to make sure they were alone. Davey tried to crawl backward like a crab, but Johnny pinned his arms with lightning speed and placed a knee on Davey's chest. He squeezed and twisted the skin on Davey's arm as he let his full weight fall onto Davey. Davey closed his eyes, squirming and wheezing.

"Say uncle," Johnny whispered.

Johnny gasped, and then Davey could breathe again. He opened his eyes and peered through the upside-down V of someone's pant legs. Johnny lay on his back, splayed out on the ground, struggling to lift his head with a woozy look on his face. Davey looked up at the person standing pretty much on top of him, their legs over his. Long, curly red hair and pale arms stuck out of a man's shirt.

It was the girl. In the same weird clothes and carrying a dirty backpack. Davey came to his senses and stood up just as Johnny scrambled to his feet. Her chin lifted like she was sizing up Johnny.

"Who in hell are you?" Johnny asked, looking her up and down with a disgusted sneer. "Wait," he added, holding up a hand, his face relaxing into a smirk. "*What* in hell are you?" He motioned at Davey behind her. "Girls do your fighting for you? Nice."

Most of the time Johnny's taunts sailed right past Davey, but this time Davey's fists curled into balls, and his cheeks grew hot.

The girl slowly walked right up to Johnny, and he pulled back, uncertain. Her arms trembled, and Davey heard a catch in her voice like she was about to cry. Her head tilted to one side.

"You...you beat up girls!"

Johnny's eyebrows shot up. "What? I haven't touched you!"

She stepped closer. Johnny stepped back.

"You hurt people," she sputtered, her voice full of tears. "People who are smaller than you." She took another step toward Johnny, and this time he didn't move back but stiffened. "What will your brother do when he finds out?"

Johnny's face fell. He started to speak, then stopped. He glanced from the girl to Davey and back again. Then he turned and, to Davey's complete shock, *ran*.

The girl turned toward him, not a tear on her face but panic instead.

"I've got to go back. Now!" She turned on her heel and spun around again, her hair whipping her in the face. "If you see my father...please, please, don't tell him!" She turned and fled.

Davey's dry mouth made him realize his jaw hung open and he shut it. "Tell him what?" he managed to yell at her back.

"That I left the grounds of the Library!" she shouted over her shoulder.

She ran along an expanse of grass that bordered a forest, toward the back of the Library. Davey's body tensed as she disappeared around the corner of the building, but he still didn't move. He didn't understand what he'd seen and heard.

"GO already!" he finally scolded himself, and he ran after her.

Davey pushed open the first door he saw. She acted really scared that she'd left the Library, so wouldn't she take the very first door she saw to get back in?

As the door closed behind him, he gazed up a set of modern, tiled stairs—not like the ones in the halls of the main floor. But then a whirring sound caught his attention off to the right. The sound grew louder as he approached a room without a door at the very end of the hallway. The noise chorused into *SHHHHHH*s like a crowd of librarians hushing people.

He poked his head into a laundry room, half a dozen dryers on one side, half a dozen washers on the other. All of them hummed or shushed. His brow creased.

Dryers? In the Library?

Why would she stop here? But as warmth settled around his shoulders, he found himself walking down the aisle, squinting through the circular windows on the washers at what looked like the dark maroon curtains that hung around the building.

He paused and put his hands on one of the dryers.

Ahhhhhh. When he was little, his ma used to wrap him in his favorite blanket, fresh from the dryer. After, the blanket turned into a cape, and he and his dad played superheroes. Who always won the fights. Who never got hurt.

Davey's heart thudded dully, and he removed his hands from the dryer. He walked to the end of the room. A dark square of an area, just big enough for a person, maybe two small ones, peeled off to the right. But no one was there.

Davey stood there a moment, thinking of how big the Library was, how many places a person could hide. Maybe she had gone back behind that locked door. The private door.

A pencil rolled out from the dark area into the light. Davey crept up to inspect it. As he bent over it, a rustling of paper made him jump, and he whipped his head in the direction of the sound.

The girl slept in a cubbyhole that he couldn't see without being right in front of it. A sketch pad sat askew in her lap, something drawn on the page.

Davey swallowed. Was this normal? Someone running so fast and then falling asleep like that? Could she be having some sort of fit?

He tiptoed up to her, nudged her shoulder with his right hand, and leapt back as if she might bite.

Her eyes snapped open. They gazed at each other in silent shock.

She looked down at the sketch pad. "Oh no," she moaned. "I did this. I got between you. There was no one to tie my hands!"

Tie her hands?

Her eyes darted wildly like she wanted to escape, but then she ripped the sketch out of the book and thrust it toward Davey.

"Would you take this? Please? And burn it as soon as you can?"

Davey gaped. "What?"

"I was stupid to butt in, but I could feel...it was like I could hear...that you needed help."

Davey bristled. "I didn't yell for help."

"I mean"—she waved her right hand, which still held a pencil—"I mean I *felt* your fear. And I just followed that feeling until I found you."

Davey stuffed his hands in his pockets. He had been a little afraid. But wait. He shook his head, trying to clear his thoughts. "That...makes no sense. And what does that have to do with you wanting me to take this drawing?"

She stood up and held it out to him again. "I shouldn't even be talking to you. Please, won't you burn this for me? Please?"

His eyes lowered to the drawing, and he took a step back.

Johnny's face stared up at him, but it was a face he'd never imagined: dark marks streaked his forehead and cheeks, his mouth hung open as if he were panting, and his eyes rolled to the side in terror of something outside the picture. He also looked half bent over, like he'd fallen or, worse, he was running on all fours.

Like something was chasing him.

Darkness also surrounded Johnny, but it was a textured kind of dark. Davey squinted. It kind of looked like...dirt?

Could Johnny be in a giant...*hole*?

"That's...super creepy," Davey murmured.

"Please?" she repeated, and as she stepped into the light, her lips trembled.

"Why?"

"Because I'll have to give it to Father to burn and he'll know. He'll know I left. And..." She hesitated. "It could mess things up. Mess up why we came here."

Her arm dropped. "If you take this and burn it, I won't bother you again." She took a shaky breath. "I mean, I shouldn't bother you again. For your sake."

Davey cocked his head to one side. "Huh?"

The pale girl swallowed hard. "I can tell you're nice, and so I thought I should warn you: I'm bad luck."

Davey exhaled sharply. "Listen." He took the page out of her hand. "I'll do what you say. I'll burn it."

Her face grew pink, and a smile tugged at the corners of her mouth.

But Davey continued, "Right after you answer every single one of my questions."

CHAPTER 6—DAVEY

98 days since the accident

Davey and the girl rode down a Library elevator.

"How come we didn't take the stairs?" Davey asked.

"I don't find this place when I take the stairs."

They passed one, two levels...6...5...the numbers said. How had he not known the main floor was the seventh floor?

"Where are we going?" he asked, watching the numbers light up as they descended.

4...3...

"To the bottom. To the basement."

"How big is this place? I grew up in Virtue, and I didn't know it had a basement!"

The girl paused before answering. "Things have been different for me too since I met you."

The elevators dinged as they reached the bottom floor.

"How come you wanna go to the basement?"

"Because people hardly ever come down here. We can talk in private. And there's so much stuff, it's kind of like a treasure hunt, even if you're by yourself."

Davey glanced at her quickly at the mention of a treasure hunt.

Just then the doors opened and Davey gasped.

"Whoa."

They stepped out of the elevator into an enormous cavern. Burnt-orange walls of craggy rock stretched and arched high over their heads, the ceiling swallowed by darkness. Faint, embedded lights pointed up from various corners, the effect soft and grainy. The far edges of the cavern melted into blackness.

Their shoes and voices echoed as they walked down a hard path toward the center of the basement. Up ahead, countless rugs lay around in all sizes and colors. Some thin, some furry, some velvety. Some patterned, some plain. On them stood clusters of lamps, wounded furniture, and lots of stuff: paperweights, a globe, fountain pen stands, heavy marble candlestick holders without candles, and stacks of dusty binders.

Davey's nose twitched at the dust hovering everywhere.

"I can't believe this is still the Library." Davey glanced at the rough walls and the dark corners, uneasy. "Are we allowed to be down here?"

"Father said I'm free to go wherever the diary is not," the girl said. "As long as I stay on the Library grounds."

"No, I mean like, the people who let me use the phone to call my mom. The staff. Would they be okay with it?" He squinted in the weak light.

"I don't know. They avoid me. Like most people. Certain people stare, but when I look at them, they pretend to be busy." She briefly angled her face toward Davey's. "You're different."

"Yeah," Davey answered dryly. His days spent underwater came back to him. *It's so great to be different.* He stopped as they reached the edge of the rugs.

The heads of their shadows quivered over shapes of furniture against the back wall.

The girl ducked under a nearby dining table and dragged two of the four furry green beanbags out from under it. "Careful, they might have holes. I flopped on one, and it leaked a bit." She pulled them to the edge of the rugs, away from the tangle of furniture and things.

She and Davey each sank into one, their legs dangling over the edges, their feet nearly touching.

Davey put his fingers on either side of his head. "I got so many questions I can't keep them straight. I think I'm just gonna remember the first day I saw you and work from there."

She nodded.

Davey looked around, rubbed his shoulders, and thought for a moment.

"That first day you said something real weird. Something about being sorry for what happened to me." He closed one eye and cocked his head to one side. "What'd you mean?"

She slid her backpack off and hugged it to her chest. "You...seemed sad. Really sad. I knew there had to be a reason for it."

"Oh." Davey sat in silence for a while. "Okay. Uh..." He paused, chewed his lip. "Say, did you, uh, know...Dr. Hathorne?"

Evil shook her head.

"It doesn't matter," he added quickly as a question formed on her face. He realized she didn't know what happened to his dad. "What I really meant to ask was, why did you move here for a diary?"

"It's temporary," the girl interjected.

"Okay," Davey continued, "but still. Wait, where did you move from?"

"Boston."

Davey gazed around the room and then perked up. "Hey, I thought I saw a globe when we came in." He slid out of the beanbag and wandered to an end table behind him that had a heavy glass globe with a crack in it. Davey struggled to see in the dim light as he slowly spun it and then traced from where they were to Boston.

His finger stopped. "Massachusetts, right?" he called over his shoulder.

"Uh-huh." She nodded.

Davey returned and sank cross-legged into the beanbag this time, smooshing it underneath his legs so he didn't topple over. "You came *across the United States* for this diary. It must be real important."

She tucked her legs under her.

"Why?" He gestured around them. "You clearly don't want anyone to know, but I won't tell."

"I know you won't," she whispered.

"Huh?" Davey asked, leaning forward.

She raised her voice. "Father's been looking for it forever. It has...answers. Answers that can...help us." She bent over, flattening herself against her legs and squeezing her backpack. She shivered. "Help *me*, I mean."

Davey stood up, removed his jacket, and threw it over her shoulders.

She shot upright as Davey returned to his beanbag.

"It is cold in here," he agreed.

The girl touched the jacket sleeve, speechless, and slowly sank onto the beanbag again.

"Can you even hint at why an old diary could help you?"

"It's kind of... I have something like...a disease. It's why I draw things like...Johnny."

"A disease makes you draw?"

She licked her lips and nodded. "And it's been a horrible burden on Father."

"Drawing? Why is drawing so hard on him?" Davey scrunched up his face in confusion.

"It's hard to explain, but it's not good. Father thinks the diary has the cure."

Davey straightened up. "A diary? Not a doctor? Ma works at the hospital, you really—"

But she shook her head and he stopped.

"A doctor can't help. Only Father. And the diary."

"A disease," Davey repeated, remembering discussions with his ma. "Viral or baxt—backeer—well, uh, is it viral?"

"If you're asking me if you can catch it, you can't."

Davey screwed his mouth to the side. "I still don't get it. How's a diary supposed to cure you?"

She didn't answer right away. Finally she said, "I trust Father." Her face took on an unfocused look, and her voice dropped into a manly tone. "Can you imagine, Evil, what would have become of you? If it weren't for me?"

Davey shrank back. "What are you doing?"

"My father. That's how he sounds to me."

"I gotta be honest. That was creepy. Have you ever talked like that...to anyone else?"

"Just myself."

"I'd keep it that way. But oh, yeah, why does he call you that...word?" Davey made a face.

Her brows furrowed. "What word?"

Davey grimaced. "*Evil.*"

"He didn't choose it; it's not his fault," she blurted.

"Didn't choose it? I heard him call you that."

The girl swallowed. "It's my name." She took a moment before going on. "My name is Evil. It's part of...the disease."

Davey's teeth began to chatter, and she stood up, pulling off Davey's jacket, but he held up a hand.

"Nah, it's okay. Keep it for now." He rubbed his nose and breathed warmth into his hands. "I'm just, uh, trying to get a handle on what you said."

She nodded, looking away. She hunched her shoulders inside Davey's jacket.

Davey pulled his legs up under his chin, resting his chin on his arms. "Okay, you said he didn't choose this name. So whaddya mean, your ma did?"

"Mother died having me." Her face remained blank.

Davey gasped. "Whoa. You never met... You never had ...?" His jaw clenched against more chattering.

"No one could do better than Father. No one."

Davey dropped his legs and leaned forward.

"But he's the one that named you Evil! How can you say he didn't choose it?"

She left her backpack behind as she pushed herself off of the beanbag. She crossed her arms and paced. "Please, just...believe me." She turned to Davey. "It's too...complicated...to explain, but he didn't want to. He *had* to."

"Complicated? It plain doesn't add up." He stood up, shoved his hands into his pants' pockets, and paced. "I think I have more questions than when we started!"

She walked over to Davey and touched his arm. He stopped pacing.

"I'm sorry." She bit her lip and looked past him as she dropped her hand. "Father said it's dangerous to explain. People won't understand." Her voice dropped into her father's again. "Look, Evil, at how people treat you once they learn your name. What do you think they'd do if they knew the truth?"

Davey winced. "Gosh, why do you do that? Imitate your dad?"

She raised her eyes to his. "I'm alone a lot. And if he's not around, I can at least...pretend he is. It helps."

"Helps you what?"

"Feel less lonely. Less upset about how things are."

He suddenly brightened. "But, hey. You said you were gonna be cured. So can you tell me what that means? Like, what happens then?"

A small, happy glow spread over her face. She leaned close and whispered.

"Father said I should practice while I'm here. Practice for when I get to be *nor*—

healthy." She exhaled. "I get a new name, any one I want. I can have friends. I won't have to draw anymore unless I want to."

"Oh man!" Davey smacked his forehead. "The drawing! Can I see it?" He pointed to his jacket pocket.

She pulled it out, offering it to him.

He unfolded it and frowned at Johnny's terrified face. He held it up to her and she turned away.

"Why'd you draw this?"

She took a step back and removed Davey's jacket, holding it out to him.

Davey's face fell as he accepted the jacket. "Did I say something wrong?"

She shook her head, backtracked to her beanbag, and pulled her backpack over her shoulders.

"Then how come I feel you're about to leave?" He pulled on the jacket.

Her eyes darted between the elevators and Davey.

"Drawings...like that...are part of the disease. Like I said."

"Huh?"

She continued to eye the elevator as she edged away from Davey.

"I mean, I can't help it. When I"—she inhaled a shaky breath—"have strong feelings,"—she exhaled noisily—"I get this urge to draw. It's really...strong. Like, I don't have a choice. The only time I can...resist...is when Father ties my hands."

"Ties you...?" Davey's eyes bulged and he shuddered. He let a silence fall for a while. Eventually he said, "I used to have a punchy clown. You know, the kind where you punch it, and it swings back at you?"

The girl nodded, creeping farther toward the path leading to the elevators.

"When I used to get upset, I would punch it in my room. I would punch it until I felt tired. And then, I felt better." He looked her in the eye. "Is that why you draw?"

She looked down. "I do it because I have to. Like breathing. Like eating. The more I try not to, the more it...hurts. I've always drawn, Davey. Since I can remember."

Davey blinked and nodded slowly, longer than he usually would.

"Okay, sounds a little stronger than my thing with Punchy the Clown." He held up the drawing to her, and she turned away from it again. "Why this one, though? And why do I have to burn it?"

"I know Johnny's a bully... I've known plenty of bullies. But I don't want anything bad to happen to him."

"You know him?" Davey asked, surprised she knew his name.

She only squared her shoulders. "If you burn it, he'll be okay."

Davey's shoulders raised and he shook his head again. "Boy am I gonna have a headache from doing that, but I can't help it. Can you...explain what you just said?"

She briefly closed her eyes, then resumed pacing; her fingers looped around her backpack straps. "I never know what I'm going to draw until it's done. I didn't plan on drawing whatever is happening to Johnny, but I know that if Father doesn't burn the drawings, they come true." She glanced at the sketch and then away. "And it's never good."

Davey slowly closed the distance between them, and she stayed put this time. He looked her dead in the eye.

"You really believe that? That...what you draw...happens in real life?"

She lowered her head, breaking eye contact.

"What did you mean about it never being good? Don't you draw other—oh wait." He did a double take. "Hey, were all those drawings yours? That I saw in that room?"

She nodded but didn't look up. "But you won't tell," she whispered.

"'Course not, there's nothing to tell." He didn't add, *Because I don't have anyone to tell.* "But...are you telling me that no matter what you draw, it happens in real life, and it turns out bad?"

The girl raised her eyes to his, and her lower lip trembled. She nodded again.

"And that only your dad can keep that from happening by burning them?"

"I can't burn it myself. I can't even be in the same room when Father burns them. Father said it's impossible for me to burn them because of my...condition. No one else has ever tried. I'm just hoping, I'm just so hoping because you're different...that maybe you could. Maybe you could burn it."

Davey glanced at the picture again before folding it up many times until it fit into the front pocket of his backpack.

She walked toward him, pleading.

"You haven't changed your mind, have you? I told you a lot more than I should have."

Davey paused for a moment before answering. "No, I—I'll do it. Like I said."

"And you'll show me the proof? The ashes?"

He hesitated again. "Sure. Sure I will."

She tilted her chin up and glanced at him from the side of her eye. "You feel different."

"It's a lot to take."

She nodded.

"But one thing. I'm not gonna call you by that name."

Her head snapped up. "But...you have to. Father—"

"No," Davey said, shaking his head. "I don't have to."

"It might affect the cure, Davey."

He folded his arms. "Calling you that name won't cure anything."

The girl bit her lip, her eyes big. She exhaled, her shoulders slumping slightly.

"Okay," she whispered.

That night, Davey walked slower than ever on the dark trip home. Lost in his thoughts, he almost ran into one of the old-fashioned black lampposts that dotted the corners of the busy parts of town. The fog didn't help, making everything hazy. One thought wore a groove in his mind, weighing him down.

She's crazy. She's crazy. She's crazy.

No matter how nice she was—and standing up to Johnny was really nice—he couldn't hang around a crazy person. He had enough troubles of his own.

Davey stopped at the corner of his street.

Oh, that's her disease. A mental disease.

Something he knew nothing about. Neither his ma nor the doctors at the hospital could cure mental diseases as far as he knew. Davey had pored over medical books for kids at one time, but none of the colored illustrations showed what a mental disease looked like.

But I promised her. I have to at least do what I said and show her the ashes.

And then what? Would he keep running into her?

Could he give up the Library to avoid her?

He closed his eyes for longer than a blink.

No way. I'm not losing the Library, too.

After he'd eaten a little dinner, he waited until his ma had been watching TV a few minutes before he quietly slipped a stool in front of the kitchen cabinets. He felt around on top of the ones closest to the fridge until his hand closed on a book of matches. He wanted the box of matches for easy striking, but he knew it was too big for his jeans pocket. Davey put the stool back in its usual place before turning out the kitchen lights and heading over to lean against the wall where the couch sat. He didn't want his ma to see his face.

"I'm, uh, gonna take a bath," he said to her profile, against which the TV lights played. His ma absently touched the gold cross around her neck, a habit that had increased since the accident. She wore her usual "after-work" attire—a cotton scarf around her head that matched a full-length, flowy dress of the same color. Burgundy today. She sewed them herself and Davey believed she had every color of the rainbow.

She turned his way, her smile lighting up her round face, and he edged back into the gloom of the small dining area.

"You feeling okay, honey?" she asked and his stomach twisted.

"Yeah. I just wanted to think."

"Oh." She reached out a hand, and he stepped toward her, gave her his. She squeezed it and, like always, he felt a little better for it. "You take your time then." She smiled warmly at him before dropping his hand, and then he knew he could scuttle in front of the TV to reach his room.

He changed into his pajamas, staring at the matchbook on his dresser.

It would only worry Ma if she knew what I was doing. Heck, even I can't believe I'm going through with this.

In the bathroom, Davey couldn't even look at himself in the mirror without rolling his eyes. He set the drawing on the counter. It looked smooth like he'd never folded it. *Special paper?* he wondered as he plugged the drain of the sink to catch the ashes. He flipped the front of the matchbook to meet the rough strip on the back and sandwiched the match in there like he'd seen adults do.

"Oh, just *do* it already," he muttered. He held the pieces of cardboard together as he whisked the match out. It flared. He swiftly picked up the sketch, held it over the sink, and lowered the match to the corner of the page.

The drawing remained intact as the fire ate the match until Davey had to drop it in the sink. He scrunched up his face. Were they old matches? He shrugged and took out another and struck it.

This time he balanced the drawing over the sink basin, dropped the lit match in the center of the paper, and stood back to watch.

The flame shriveled the match until it crumbled to ash, but the picture looked untouched.

Davey grabbed the drawing, held it up to the light. He couldn't detect any damage.

He now crumpled the paper, then tossed it into the sink. He lit one, two, three, four matches, dropping each into the basin on top of the crumpled sketch.

One by one, the matches flamed, blackened, and shrank, but the drawing looked the same. Davey's mouth went dry as he gingerly picked up the drawing and spread it out on the countertop. As he smoothed it, the wrinkles disappeared under his hand like he'd never balled it up at all.

He examined both sides, but he couldn't find even a hint of brown or a burn hole.

Davey threw the drawing into the basin and slapped the faucet on.

The water poured over the paper, pooling around it until it floated. Davey turned the water off, then used both hands to push the sketch under the water, flattening it against the basin.

He pulled the drawing out of the water and stretched it between his hands.

Johnny's horror-struck face stared back at him. The paper wasn't even damp.

He lowered the drawing, and his eyes found his own in his reflection. He swallowed hard, willing his teeth not to chatter with the fear that crept up his spine.

Now who's crazy?

CHAPTER 7—EVIL

6 days until the Anniversary

After Davey left the Library and Evil had eaten dinner with her father, she retreated to her room and changed into one of her father's old shirts, her usual nightgown. She grabbed her well-worn copy of *Grimm's Fairy Tales* from her suitcase under the cot. She'd memorized the book long ago, but the dainty, detailed drawings and soft colors usually soothed her.

Now, however, Evil stared at the cover without opening it and finally put it on the wooden TV tray that served as her nightstand.

She turned out the lights and lay on top of the covers, looking at the ceiling, not seeing the curling paper and sketches of faces but thinking about Davey. How his eyes had changed. How the way he *felt* had changed. Now he felt more like...

Everyone else.

Not completely, but there had been a shift. Why? Memories flashed in her mind, the boys and girls who had looked at her that way, teased her, bullied her...but Davey wasn't like that.

A muffled yell caused her to bolt upright. Evil leapt out of bed, flinging open her bedroom door and running down the hall as a second yell erupted from nearby.

She sprinted toward the noise, flung open the connecting door, and rounded the corner at the end of the hall, ignoring the looks of various tourists lingering nearby. She headed toward the row of offices to the side of the main desk area and skidded to a halt when she saw the collection of people who briefly turned to stare at her. One man with dark brown hair that brushed his shoulders and deep circles under his large eyes continued to stare long after the others turned their attention back to whatever was happening. Evil found she couldn't look away until he, too, turned around.

Moans came from where they crowded.

"I came into work at this hour to have some privacy from the leering Reverend Mather! And I was wearing gloves, for God's sake, so how does this happen?"

Evil recognized the voice of Lawrence, the primary antiquarian of the diary (she privately called him Fishy Lawrence). Lawrence's cranky, gravelly voice could be heard somewhere at least once a day. She thought of the drawing her father asked her to do, something that would keep Lawrence from reading the diary. Her hands grew cold, and she pulled her father's long sleeves over them.

Evil crept up to the fixated crowd and kneeled down at an open sliver beside someone's legs. Lawrence stood holding out his red, welted hands, his face half turned away as if he couldn't look directly at them. Across from him stood a tall woman, her back to Evil. A thick, coffee-colored braid cascaded down her back. She wore a loose black dress that fell lightly to her ankles, followed by a pair of lace-up flat-heeled black boots. The woman briefly dipped her head and put an inhaler to her lips, sucked in a quick breath, and then looked up as she tucked it back into her dress pocket. The tall figure turned her head slowly, revealing huge, dark eyes full of hurt. For a moment Evil forgot about Lawrence, caught up in the sight of someone both sad and pretty like a black and white photograph. The woman's left eyebrow shot up at Evil, and Lawrence abruptly stopped talking, following the woman's gaze.

Evil gasped when Lawrence caught sight of her. Her face reddened, suddenly aware that she'd left the apartment in only an oversized shirt. Evil ducked her head and sprinted down the hall. His voice trailed after her.

"And there's his...evil spawn! I have no allergy—these pages must have been dusted with a toxic chemical, and why on earth would that be the case? You cannot pay me enough to continue working on this cursed diary, Ms. Goode! I demand a new assignment!"

His words weighed on Evil's chest. It *had* been too much, just like Father feared. She had to tell Father. Better to tell him than have him find out.

As she made her way back to their living quarters, something pricked at Evil's memory. *Ms. Goode...I know that name.* When they first arrived a few months ago, Evil had fallen asleep curled up in a chair near a vent in the Children's Realm. Faint as it was, her father's voice floated up through the vent, startling her awake. He was yelling.

"Ms. Goode, you are the head librarian. How can you not know the whereabouts of my boxes? Is this Library not under your control? Do you have thieves among your staff?"

Her father hadn't mentioned any missing boxes to her, but they must be important for him to yell like that.

Back in their living quarters, Evil couldn't find her father in his study or bedroom.

And he hadn't been with Lawrence...but based on what Lawrence said, Father hadn't known he'd be working on the diary.

Evil went back to her room, wriggled into her pants, and winced as she laced the outgrown sneakers. She leaned against the frame of her door, tugging on a strand of hair.

He could be anywhere. She spent most days exploring the Library, and every day, she found a new path, a new room, a new stairway.

She sped out of her room and down the hall. Closing the door marked Private behind her, she explored the other hallways right alongside hers. The doors at the end had signs on them:

Closed for Construction.

Closed for Maintenance.

Evil frowned and made her way out to the main desk. The staff glanced up and looked hurriedly away. She walked toward a set of large double doors on the opposite end of the Library.

Closed for Special Event.

Evil put her hands on her hips and narrowed her eyes. She grasped the handle of the doors, but they didn't give, so she turned toward the back of the Library. She'd seen another door there, past the reading rooms.

When she reached the door, it only said Pottery Classes Resume Next Wednesday.

Evil pushed the door handle and, to her surprise, it gave. When she opened it fully, she stared at a gray cement wall with a small electric candle sitting in a carved out arch. Evil frowned, puzzled, then looked right—another wall—and then left: a set of stairs going down.

Evil didn't go down the steps right away. The faint light produced by the candle faded quickly at the curve of the stairs. Only a handful of steps into the tight passageway, the stairway sloped and veered away so she couldn't even see the door above her anymore.

Evil passed another electric candle at the next landing that flickered like a real one, making the shadows dance.

"It's just a candle," Evil said out loud as she gave the shadows a wary glance. The air grew colder as she made her way down, and she rubbed her hands together. She touched the rough wall as she rounded another curve, and it chilled her fingers. She couldn't hear anything but the tread of her sneakers on the stone stairs.

At some point she stopped and looked up, taking in the darkness, shifting shadows, and twisting steps above her. She licked her lips and sang rhymes in her head with each step.

One, two, three, four, will I ever reach the floor? Five, six, seven, eight, will Father be mad that I stayed up late?

As she reached fifty, the stairs rounded again but this time abruptly ended at a tall arched wooden door. This door looked like something that should've been attached to a fence: slats of unpainted wood and a round, iron handle that had to be twisted to open.

When she opened the door, Evil blinked into the darkness of a hall. A grainy light appeared ahead. She scurried toward it and entered a bright room with a ceiling that soared many floors above her head. A huge structure she'd never seen before sat in the center. It smelled like smoke.

The tall, cylindrical brick structure punched right through the ceiling so Evil didn't know where it ended. Four sets of steps led up to its entrance, and the golden interior light shone on vases and figures on shelves. Black stacks of something that reminded her of tires full of holes stood around the structure. Curious, she took a step toward the tower when a familiar sound distracted her.

"Listen, dammit to hell!"

She turned her head toward her father's voice, relieved and anxious at the same time. She'd never heard him say words like that. She walked toward the sound with a soft tread, making her way in the direction of his voice. A door stood slightly ajar from the stone wall that ran beside the brick structure. She tiptoed up to it and peered inside.

Her father bent over some kind of worktable. He wore a dirty white apron smeared with gray streaks. A large bag full of sludgy stuff sat to the right of him. Her eyes widened at the various tiny statues that stood before him. He held one in his hand, petting it. With his other hand, he touched the silver Mather crest around his neck. Then she remembered.

Pottery Class...he's sculpting, not petting.

She'd been very young when she caught him in their basement back home, his fingers covered in something sticky and gray with an earthy smell. She was so small that he hadn't seen her watching him from the door. He'd gripped statues slightly larger than Barbie dolls in his hands, and more surrounded him on shelves that ran from floor to ceiling. He'd been crying and whispering to the ceiling, *"Why? Why have you forsaken me?"* Her father's tears had so alarmed her that she tried hard to forget what she'd seen. But she couldn't.

All the statues were of her. All the way back to when she was a baby.

After that, he never went to the basement to sculpt again, as far as Evil knew.

The statues she saw now mirrored her memory. And real—each one looked so real—with tiny, detailed hands, wrinkles in their clothing. One was of a tall woman in black with a long braid down her back. It reminded her of Ms. Goode, the woman Lawrence had yelled at. The figure in her father's hands also looked familiar. Hands stuffed in pockets, shaggy, curly hair...

She squinted hard and then gasped as she recognized the statue he held.

Her father's eyes locked on her.

For a moment, Evil's limbs froze beneath his gaze, a look of such loathing that she forgot to breathe.

Then he closed his eyes again, and when he opened them, his face looked normal. Serious, but kind and concerned.

As he laid down the figure and went to her, Evil fought the urge to run.

It's Father. He loves me. He knows me. He loves me.

She stepped back as he gently pushed open the door and then closed it behind him. He kneeled down to her and took her chilled hands into his own.

"I locked that door to this area, you know. The one that led you into here? I have the key in my pocket." He sighed and smiled, but it was a small smile, and Evil wished she hadn't come.

"But you're special, of course. You know how I told you to practice being normal for when the Curse is over?"

She nodded, still shaken and unsure of what to say.

"I'm practicing too. For after the Curse. I have to be prepared."

"But what are you doing?" she croaked.

He stood, dropping her hands. "It will make sense in time. After I read the diary, I can explain it."

The diary...

Evil found her voice. "Father, Lawrence, his hands... It was too much, like you feared. I don't think he'll be working on the diary anymore."

To her relief, he smiled again.

"I wasn't overly fond of him anyway, Evil. Perhaps I can help them find someone better. Now go back to bed, and I'll be up soon to check on you." He pulled her to his side in a half hug and then released her.

The Reverend then disappeared back into the room. This time he shut the door all the way.

Even though it took longer to go up the stairs and Evil had to take multiple breaks, sometimes even sitting on the cold stone, it didn't bother her. The shadows didn't spook her this time. She couldn't stop thinking about what she'd seen. Her skin grew icy and stayed that way, even after she curled into a ball under a blanket on her cot.

Her heart beat fast, too fast to fall asleep for a long time. And every beat whispered a name:

Davey, Davey, Davey...

Why was her father making a statue of Davey?

CHAPTER 8—DAVEY

99 days since the accident

For the first time since the accident, Davey didn't think about his dad right before he went to bed. Instead, he thought of how the drawing wouldn't burn just a few hours ago. He worried about the picture of Johnny he'd slid underneath the couch, too spooked to have it in his own room. His stomach flip-flopped at the thought that it was even in the apartment.

Something's wrong with that drawing. Something bad.

He shook his head against his pillow and clutched at the sheet in frustration. He didn't want to believe what Ava said about the pictures coming to life; that was—

His train of thought screeched to a halt.

Ava?

Davey recognized the name from his favorite childhood poem, "Ava and Arthur." His ma had worried it would give him nightmares, but he couldn't get enough of it.

Ava and Arthur loved to make tea,
and drink in their sailboat while out on the sea.

They had great adventures on foreign lands full of pirates, monsters, and evil magicians. Ava drowns trying to save Arthur during a storm, and he continues to sail, determined to undo time as he searches for her in other lands.

She and the sea embraced as one,
Forever and ever, 'til time was undone.
"I will sail past forever, for my love endures,
because you are mine, just as I am yours."

Davey grimaced. The name was special, and he barely knew this girl. But he wasn't going to call her "Evil" if he had to see her again.

And he had to, didn't he?

He shifted in bed. She'd asked to see the ashes. She wanted proof.

How would this affect her disease to know it hadn't worked? Would it be best to avoid her? But if he wanted to go back to the Library, which he did, how would he manage it?

His father's voice echoed in his head: *"Son, do you want to be her friend or not? Decide that and you'll know what to do."*

Friend? Davey turned on his left side and stared at his bookcase. *The Great Big Anatomy Book for Kids* dominated the top shelf, the best present he ever got from his mom. He used to pore over the illustrations of muscles and organs for hours. He hadn't looked at it since the accident.

He hadn't done a lot since the accident. He hadn't *felt* a lot either.

Why did you have to die?

He chewed on his lower lip, trying to block out the endless question.

Ava made him feel. He could almost be himself with her. Almost like before the accident.

But there was more. Davey couldn't quite get a hold on it. Ava, the diary...Dr. Hathorne. Maybe...maybe this diary had answers for both of them? He squirmed under the covers. Trying to understand why his dad had died was like poking a cut that hadn't healed. If he could leave it alone, maybe it would get better on its own. Somehow.

Ava. He sighed. He did have to call her by a name. He just wished his brain wasn't stuck on that one.

He flopped onto his back and focused on the stucco ceiling that reminded him of dollops of white frosting hanging over his head.

Telling her that he couldn't burn the drawing was the honest thing to do, but maybe there was a safer way to do it... maybe with an adult around... one of the Library staff? Maybe—

The scream of a siren in the distance cut into his thoughts. The town of Virtue was small enough that it wasn't something you heard every night. And it only made him think of one thing.

Davey pulled the covers over his head.

The next day, Davey didn't see Johnny at school. Groups of kids huddled on the playground, whispering his name, but he couldn't catch the details. The drawing felt hot in his backpack, though he knew that couldn't be true. Or, at least, he hoped it wasn't true.

After school, Davey headed off to the Library. He and the girl—*Ava*, he mentally practiced—had agreed to meet under the white rabbit's pocket watch. He hadn't gone that far beyond the elementary school when he came upon a large group of kids crossing the street. A cluster of girls passed him, whispering. He recognized a girl with straight blonde hair and a turned-up nose from his fifth-grade class last year.

"Hey," he called. The whole group turned their heads. They eyed him and then turned away, except for the blonde girl.

"Hey." She offered a wary smile when he'd caught up to her.

"Uh, so, what's going on?"

Her eyebrows arched. "You don't know?"

Davey shook his head.

She lowered her voice. "It's Johnny. Something happened at the cemetery last night. They think it was his brother. Like he played a trick on Johnny and...something went wrong." She paused and looked over her shoulder at her friends up ahead. She edged toward the curb. "I have to catch up with them..."

"Wait!" Davey begged, stepping forward. "Where's everyone going?"

She leaned toward him, cupped her hand around her mouth, and whispered.

"They say there's blood near Dr. Hathorne's crypt. Johnny's blood."

Time slowed for Davey as the girl ran for her friends without saying goodbye. His mouth tasted cottony.

Then time sped back up and so did his heart. He ran all the way to the Library.

Davey pounded up the front steps as best he could, raced through the Time Tunnel to the protests of tourists, and burst through the double doors. Startled faces of the Library staff looked his way. He slowed down because his chest hurt. By the time he made it to the top of the spiral staircase that led to the Children's Realm, he gripped the thick wooden railing as if he might topple over the side.

His heart galloped—and not just from running. He didn't want to believe Ava, didn't want to give her disease power by handing over the drawing. And now this news about Johnny...

"Davey," his father said in his head. *"What did I always say about solving a crime?"*

Don't settle on a theory until there's proof.

Davey stopped on a stair. *Theory #1: Ava's drawing was not normal.* He had proof of that.

As tourists moved around him, some casting long looks his direction, Davey began to climb again.

Theory #2: Ava's drawing caused something bad to happen to Johnny. That needed proof.

But the memory of Ava's words made his skin prickle. *"What will your brother do when he finds out?"*

He reached the rainbow arch at the top of the stairs. His heart thumped eagerly like it always did, but his stomach twisted with anxiety. His feet dragged on the spongy yellow brick road. In the stacks of books and displays, he bumped into a bunch of girls wearing braids and whispering around some dumb old-fashioned bag on a bench.

Toddlers played under a tall, multicolored Truffula Tree, which Davey thought was a dandelion made of candy until he read the book. He absently nodded to Charlotte in her web, woven in a small room turned into a barn stall. Probably the 8th Charlotte since he'd been going to the Realm? So cool she was real, though. At last, he spotted the glint of the rabbit's brassy pocket watch. The way it hung from a high shelf turning back and forth always mesmerized him.

As she'd promised, Ava sat cross-legged on the floor on the other side of the shelves from where the watch hung. Her backpack lay beside her along with a large book spread out on the floor. She stared at an illustration of a sleeping girl with red lips and golden hair surrounded by thorns that cradled her with their sharp tips. Davey couldn't tell where the girl's hair ended and the strange thorns began.

Ava's head snapped up. She quickly closed the book.

"I didn't hear you."

"I used to get lost in books too. I wish—" He caught himself, not wanting to admit he hadn't been able to do that since the accident. He shook his head and cleared his throat. "Do you wanna head to the basement again? So I can explain? I mean, if we won't get in trouble?"

Ava drew the large book to her chest like a shield. "Something's wrong, isn't it? Because if you just had to hand over ashes, you wouldn't need to explain anything."

Davey made a mental note. *Never try to lie to Ava.*

He grimaced. "It's complicated."

She stood up, still clutching the book. "What did you do with the drawing?"

Davey unzipped his backpack and handed it to her. He'd rolled it up this time. "I tried to do what you said. It just...didn't work."

"What happened?" Ava accepted it with a trembling hand.

Davey cast an uneasy glance around him as kids wandered past.

"I mean," he whispered, "I couldn't destroy it. I tried. It...won't burn or anything. It kinda seemed...indestructible."

The paper made a rustling sound as Ava's shaking hand unrolled it. She stared at it, breathing fast. Her eyes lifted to meet Davey's.

"Do you know... Do you know if Johnny's...okay?"

Davey turned his face away, remembering his recent mental note. "Uh, I wouldn't think about him right now."

Ava squeezed her eyes shut.

Davey turned to briefly eye the pocket watch. The motion calmed him. "Don't ask me to say more, okay?"

Ava let the one side of the drawing go, and it rolled back up. Sadness pulled on the corners of her mouth, her eyes, even her shoulders. She nodded slowly.

Then panic broke out over her face as she looked at the drawing in her hand. She clenched it to her chest and turned to Davey, her face pleading.

"If Father finds out... Davey, help me hide this!"

As Ava had promised, no one said a word as they made their way toward the elevators that led to the underground floors. When Davey chanced a glimpse at the staff, an elderly woman ducked her head, and others cleared their throats and turned away.

As they passed the collection of desks in the center of the Library, Davey followed Ava's gaze to a librarian dressed in all black. The woman pored over some large notebooks, and her super-long braid trailed over her shoulder. As Davey and Ava passed, she alone looked up and locked eyes with Ava.

"You know her?" Davey asked.

"That's Ms. Goode." Ava quieted her voice. "Father doesn't like her."

Davey could imagine Ava's father didn't like a lot of people. He waited until they were descending on the elevator to say what he really wanted to say.

"Didn't ya know your drawings were indestructible?"

Ava shook her head. "Father can destroy them."

"But why would it matter who is trying to destroy them?" Davey persisted. "Fire's fire no matter who lights the match."

"Father is special. He understands my...condition...better than anyone."

"But what does your condition have to do with him being able to burn them? I don't get it."

Ava didn't answer right away. "He can do...lots of things...I don't understand. He's the last living Mather."

Davey cocked his head. "Aren't you a Mather too?"

Ava's mouth turned down. "Father has always said that he's the last."

Davey decided to drop that issue.

The doors chimed and opened to the basement floor. Davey silently followed Ava. He looked around in awe of the cavern once more but cowered a little at the darkness above him.

Davey finally broke the silence as they reached the Floor of Many Rugs.

"Um, so, do you have any idea of where you want to hide it?"

Ava's arms flopped at her sides. "No," she sighed. "I don't think many people come down here, so I thought this was the best place."

She turned to Davey and pointed with the drawing. "You can take the right side, and I'll take the left. Tell me if you see a good hiding place."

Davey waded into the Land of Broken Lamps, weaving in and around them, then crawling under a large table and standing among other furniture and some boxes. He looked at a gray box next to a green velvet-covered stool that had a slash in the fabric. He stepped over the stool and squeezed past a library cart that tilted to one side. Beside the cart, an old door lay on the floor, the panes of glass that used to be in the upper part missing.

The sound of Ava's gasp rolled around the big open space, and Davey turned so fast he bumped into a stack of binders, and the upper half toppled onto other boxes beneath it.

"What? What is it?" Davey shouted as he retraced his steps over the boxes and around the furniture, his voice bouncing off the cavern walls. Ava stood in a semicircle of wingback chairs facing away from Davey, staring at something. Davey navigated another obstacle course and then edged around the chairs until they opened up to where Ava stood.

"What is it?" Davey repeated. He walked up to her and peered over her shoulder.

A regular cardboard box sat in front of her with the words *EVIL—DO NOT OPEN* in large block letters on the top. Several other boxes around it said the same thing.

"It's Father's handwriting," Ava whispered. "I... I think I've found his lost boxes!" Her face lit up with hope. "He yelled at Ms. Goode for losing them and we've found them!"

"Why would they be down here?"

"I don't know. But I can't wait to tell him; he'll be so happy. He seemed really worried when he was talking to Ms. Goode." She jumped a little with excitement, still holding the drawing of Johnny to her chest.

"Hey, but these are yours," Davey pointed out. "Did you know they were missing?"

"No. I didn't bring much."

"Well, let's open them."

Ava straightened up, and her brows drew together. "The label says not to open them."

"Nah." Davey pointed. "It just means someone who isn't you can't open them. If *you* were not supposed to open them, it would be a comma or a colon after your name, not a dash."

Ava stared at Davey, a look of wonder on her face.

Davey shoved his hands in his pockets. "Ma can be pretty serious about schooling me."

Ava pointed at the box nearest to her feet. "I don't have anything to open it with. And there's a lot of tape."

"I saw a broken fountain pen over here, and the point looked pretty sharp. Lemme go get it." Davey tripped and stumbled his way over to the long table that held pens and books and all sorts of trash and treasure on it. He grabbed the fountain pen and a couple more sharp ink pens to boot.

He and Ava poked holes in the tape on either side and peeled the sticky remains away with their fingers. Davey ran the sharp end of the fountain pen across the top, slicing through the first, then second, then third layer of tape.

"Your dad's serious about packing." Davey stood up. "Well, you can open it now."

Ava parted the cardboard sides. A layer of black shapes sat on top. Ava touched one.

"It's...metal... Iron, maybe?" She lifted one and set it back down, the side of it clanking against its twin.

"Yeah, but what is it?" Davey asked, his face scrunched up in confusion.

"It's..." Ava began, running her hand along one. "Oh. It's the Mather family crest." She picked one up and held it out to Davey.

His hand gave with the weight. "Whoa, yeah, this is heavy stuff." He examined the interlocking geometric shapes. "But are these yours?"

Ava shook her head, then touched the spot where the object had lain in the box. "I don't think that's all that's in here." She removed a few more of the crests and felt around the blank area, which was just as black as the crests.

She wrinkled her nose. "This feels like paper." She lifted up a black corner a little, then flipped through what sounded like pages in a book. She leaned in and squinted before her lips parted.

Ava flung herself backward, crashing into the chairs.

"What is it? What's in there?" Davey shouted, backing away. Without taking his eyes off of the box, he then whispered over his shoulder, his heart pounding, "What is it? Did something bite you?"

Ava took rasping breaths behind him but said nothing. Davey glanced back at her. She panted, tears running down her face as she stared at the box.

She rolled up the Johnny drawing and used it to point to the box. The rolled-up paper shook.

"Drawings. The box is full of drawings." Ava's hoarse whisper scuttled across the basement.

"Huh?" His eyes flicked between the box and Ava. "A drawing scared you that bad?"

Ava nodded, mute, fresh tears dribbling down her cheeks.

"That box," she gasped. Davey moved toward her, but she held up her free hand. She brought her hand to her chest. "Those are the drawings my father said he burned to keep them from coming true."

CHAPTER 9—EVIL

4 days until the Anniversary

Time blurred after Evil found the drawings.

She taped the Johnny picture to the back of one of the drawings on her wall later that night. If for any reason her father removed the drawing, it felt a little thicker than usual, but the back was plain.

If only I'd thought of that before, then I wouldn't have found the boxes. I wouldn't know...

Her teachers said knowledge was important, but Evil's world bent and wavered like it might break with what she'd discovered. She pled a stomachache to avoid eating dinner with her father. And she avoided him as much as possible the next day.

The following night, after discussing more of what happened with Davey after he dropped by after school, she joined her father at the dining table. Evil chewed and chewed but couldn't swallow the pasta or any of the vegetables. She spit the food into her napkin and stared across the table.

The Reverend put down his steak knife and looked up. The light caught the Mather crest around his neck.

"Is something wrong, Evil?"

"I still don't feel well." Evil's voice came out hoarse, probably from the hours of crying. She swallowed hard, pushing down her questions.

Why did you tell me you burned them? Why did you lie? All this time? All these years?

Evil cleared her throat. "May I be excused?"

68

The Reverend hesitated, then pushed back his chair and placed his linen napkin on the table. He walked over to Evil and awkwardly laid the back of his right hand against her forehead, just like their nanny-maids did. She clenched her jaw to keep from stiffening at his touch.

"You're not feverish. Did you eat something bad?"

"I...ate some of our leftovers from the Italian takeout." Her cheeks grew warm at the lie. Why did lying bother her when it didn't bother him?

Would he know? Could he tell?

"Italian!" He sat back, brow furrowed. "That was from a week ago; I thought I'd thrown it all out. Stay here."

He left, and she heard his bedroom door open, then his interior bathroom door. He returned shortly and put two white tablets by her plate.

"Chew them up and you'll probably feel better within the hour. You are free to go to your room." He returned to his plate, cutting up his steak.

Evil had chewed up these pills many times when her father had given them to the nanny-maids for her. They didn't taste bad. They did make her feel better. But she couldn't stop staring at them.

They were just normal pills, weren't they?

The sound of metal scraping against porcelain stopped again. Her eyes flicked his way. Evil's father chewed without looking away from her.

"Perhaps you are feverish. Your cheeks have color." He swallowed. "You haven't touched the pills." He laid his knife on the side of the plate and raised his chin, regarding her through half-lowered lids. "Has anything else happened, Evil?"

Evil focused on the pills again and shook her head. The heat from her cheeks spread to her neck and chest.

His fork clinked as he laid it down. A trickle of sweat ran down her back.

This was how she acted when she didn't want to tell her father the truth. And he knew it.

He sighed. "I know you wouldn't hesitate to tell me if you'd drawn a picture I should see."

Hot streams of perspiration ran down her sides.

"So it must be something else."

She still hadn't lifted her head, but the sound of wood pushing against the rug told her he'd pushed his chair back again.

"Did you...happen to engage a librarian named Ms. Goode?"

Evil's head snapped up in shock.

He doesn't know... He doesn't know anything that happened! Why would he?

But he took her reaction to mean he was right. The Reverend's face contorted, and he slammed his fist into the table. Evil yelped. His face immediately softened.

"I'm sorry, Evil. That wasn't very nice of me, was it?" He swiftly carried his chair over to her side and sat down. Very close to her.

"Tell me. *Everything.*"

The lie poured out of Evil's mouth as if it had been scalding her, pulling on memories of how adults spoke at school. She had to tell him something.

"She... took me aside today and...and... said to tell my father when I see him—since he's too busy to see her—that he is not allowed to use the Library as his own...playground."

The Reverend's hands curled into fists against his legs.

"The...clay...is for students. So is the..." Understanding swept over Evil. "Oven!"

That's what it was. All that brick, that smoky smell.

She dared to raise her eyes to her father's. His mouth formed a single hard line, and his face had turned such a deep red, Evil found herself thinking of cherries.

"Blame the witches, blame the Curse!" he growled through his teeth.

Evil's pulse throbbed. *What have I done to Ms. Goode? What will happen when he realizes I lied?*

Then he looked at Evil and exhaled. The purplish-red color faded a little.

"I'm sorry you had to experience that, Evil. An adult who conducts business through children is not to be trusted." He drummed his fingers on the table. "I'll take care of this tomorrow, assuming she's working then. But tonight, Evil, tonight I will work toward your cure." He leaned down to her, his smile suddenly boyish. "I found several books here that will help me understand the diary."

For a moment all the lies fell away, and hope made Evil's heart leap. "You did?"

"Yes!" He grabbed her hands and covered them with his. They felt rough and cool...like always. He squeezed her hands before letting them go. "So try not to disturb me tonight unless you must? I'll be in my workshop quite late, I'm sure."

"Your workshop? Downstairs?"

"Yes, I find it's very quiet, very easy to concentrate down there. I'll be leaving momentarily." With another grin, he leapt up and went straight to his study. A lock clicked after he shut the door.

The Reverend's plate sat on the table, several pieces of meat still there, a glass half-full of red wine beside it.

He's forgotten where we are. No nanny-maid to clean up after him. No kitchen at all.

Evil poured out the wine in the bathroom sink. As she scraped the meat into the garbage they stored in a broom closet in the hall, a thought so chilling crept into her mind that the plate slipped from her fingers. It thudded dully on the thick carpet. She gripped the handle of the knife until she couldn't feel her hand.

What if the cure was a lie too?

Her stomach rumbled once she was in her bed, even though it was way too early to fall asleep. Evil clasped the sides of the bed, her heart suddenly a wild bird trying to break free of a cage.

What is real? What is real? What is real?

She closed her eyes as the room spun, and she grabbed the cot even tighter.

If I let go, I'll go flying, flying into nowhere...

Not flying. Flung. She'd seen a carnival ride from a distance one time, and as it spun, she imagined people scattering to the winds in all directions.

That's how she felt. And she wanted off. Now.

She opened her eyes and willed the room to stop spinning by taking slow, deep breaths like her father had taught her to do when she was upset. She breathed in, out. In, out.

The room slowed. She sat up. Evil swung her legs to the floor.

The room stopped.

She couldn't allow herself to question *everything*; she just couldn't. To her surprise, Davey didn't want to believe her father had done anything wrong when they discussed it earlier today.

"If he fibbed, then maybe he had a good reason."

"But Davey, he said burning them was his way of helping me. He said he burned them so they wouldn't come true."

All the times her classmates had accidents, fell sick, suddenly moved away...her father had said they had to be just coincidences because he'd burnt the drawings.

Davey had persisted. "How did you feel when he said he'd done it? Burned them?"

No one had ever asked her that. Evil remembered the last time she'd brought her father a drawing to burn, almost two years ago, since her father learned to tie her hands and shape her feelings toward something else. She'd also gotten so good at shutting off her feelings. Until Davey.

"It... It hurts. Because they're... The drawings are..." Her tongue had searched for the words and curled around them. "Part of me."

"Oh." Davey had deflated, his shoulders sagging.

The rest of the memory had surfaced. "But then, another part of me feels better."

Davey had cocked his head to one side.

"Because by burning them, Father kept me from hurting anyone. I thought."

Davey had pounced on what she said. "So in the end, it did make you feel a little better?"

Evil had nodded, reluctantly.

Davey's triumphant grin soon faded, though.

"'Course," he went on, "we might have solved the mystery of why he fibbed, but not why your sketches can't be destroyed."

But what plagued Evil was not about her indestructible sketches. It was that her father had lied. It didn't matter why. Evil had one very clear memory of one thing he said over and over:

"We must always be honest with each other, Evil. Trust is all we have. Without that, all is lost."

She'd always told him everything. Even now, she wanted to find him and shout, "Why did you lie? Tell me right now! Why?"

But then why should she believe anything he would say back to her? A liar couldn't be trusted...right?

Davey's explanation made sense, but it didn't *feel* right. Just like Davey didn't *feel* right about her real name, she realized with a start.

But now she'd lied too. Was she as bad as her father? Evil covered her eyes, wondering if she had the courage to seek out Ms. Goode before her father did. She had to, she decided. She couldn't let Ms. Goode get punished for her lie. The thought made her sick and excited all at the same time. Evil had never thought this way before. Most of it felt wrong, horribly wrong, to lie. A tiny part of her, however, did open up. A small portion of her pressed her face against the bars she'd thought protected her and sucked in cool air from outside.

The lie was a decision she'd made without her father. For the first time.

All at once the nervous energy drained from her. She stood up, wobbly, staggered to the wall, and hit the light. Evil flopped back onto her bed and didn't even think of cracking a book. Her heart slowed, her eyelids hung heavily, and she drifted down, down, straight into her recurring dream.

The sharp breeze cut through her rags, so biting her teeth rattled, but she wouldn't give the crowd what it wanted. She wouldn't rub her arms, mew pitifully like an unwanted kitten. Many of the faces that gazed up at her showed eagerness. Others tried to condemn her with their grim, pious, "shouldn't you be ashamed of yourself" looks. But none of that mattered. Only one person mattered. Her eyes locked on the black-robed man who trotted on the horse in the distance. She gritted her teeth, and they ached and cracked from all the time in prison with hardly any food. She might not have witchcraft like they accused, but she did have one thing: hate.

Hate gathered like a ball of fire in the core of her being, spreading throughout her limbs, warming her. To stoke it, she squeezed the upper part of her right arm, tears springing to her eyes at the pain that splintered in all directions. She forced herself to look at the brand, and her loathing exploded, the sight of it causing the fire to course madly through her, giving her the strength to raise her arm, point a shaky hand at the man on the horse and—

Evil's own scream ripped her from the dream, and she woke up fully just as she'd flung herself at her bedroom door. Wiping the sweat from her forehead, she checked her arm: no brand. Had she really screamed?

Evil leaned against the door, shaking and sweating. The dream had changed, backed up in time a little. It seemed different.

Evil felt a tug inside her, a pull she could not resist. Her fingers itched and tingled. She stared at her hands in shock—this had never happened after the dreams. She grabbed her backpack from where she'd dropped it beside the door and withdrew her sketchbook. She slid down the wall, right where she was, both hands clutching pencils. She'd barely closed her eyes and begun the slow, rhythmic breathing when her hands swooped around the page in different directions. Her mind zipped up in a dark velvety bag as the drawings took over and told their story through her hands.

When she finally opened her eyes, her fingers ached. The point on the pencils had become flat and dull. She released the pencils from both hands, but her hands remained frozen in bird-beak shapes. She flexed her fingers and gasped with relief, then she gazed around her. Swirls and jagged slashes splashed across dozens and dozens of pieces of paper around her. No people, just...shadows. All the pages looked like splashes of dusk. Relief ran through her: no people, no frightened faces screaming from the pages.

But...what did these shadow drawings mean, then?

CHAPTER 10—DAVEY

100 days since the accident

Davey decided to eat dinner with his ma, blushing when her face showed surprise as he set the table like he used to. It felt good to pretend to be normal. After dinner they "rocked their meal away" in rocking chairs, a tradition his ma invented. Davey claimed he was too old for this when he turned eleven last year, but he didn't want to admit to himself that it calmed him down.

Davey kept thinking about what happened with Ava. He just didn't know how to make his ma understand. It sounded too weird, too scary, even to him. But he also itched to talk about it.

"Ma, how do you know when someone's lying to you?"

Her rocker stopped creaking. She stared at him with a serious expression. It looked so strange because usually a smile lit up her face like the sun. Even when he heard her crying in her room sometimes, since the accident, she always came out with a smile for him. His ma was the most popular nurse at the hospital, and he was pretty sure everyone there smelled a little bit like her cinnamon lotion at the end of her shift from her hugs.

"Who do you think's been lying to you?"

"Oh, not me, a friend—" He stopped. He couldn't believe he'd said it.

"A friend!" she echoed and started rocking again with such gusto Davey hoped the wood would hold up given his ma's size. "Well! You and Billy talking again? Or Jeff?"

Davey watched his feet push away from the floor when she said those names. Back and forth, back and forth. Names from before. Ava was now. But how could he explain?

"I keep running into this girl at the Library."

The creaking stopped again. "A girl?"

"She...likes Ray Bradbury."

"A girl," his ma repeated. "She's a friend?"

"Yeah. I guess. I mean, she's nice and we both like to read. And," he added, "we both really like the Library."

The creaking began again.

"I know how much you like it, honey." His ma sighed, wiping the corners of her eyes. "That sounds like a budding friendship alright. But you said something about lying? Is someone lying to that girl?"

Now Davey stopped rocking. "Actually, I think we both know they're lying. I guess the problem is deciding if it's for a good reason or a bad reason. How can you tell?"

His ma touched the small gold cross she wore around her neck. "How does it feel in her heart? Figure that out and there's her answer."

Oh. Davey knew how Ava felt about being lied to. But he'd argued with her because... why? He heard Ava's father's voice calling her "Evil," saw his stern face again. Why would he stand up for someone like that?

On Wednesday, Davey and Ava had arranged to meet somewhere more private than the spot under the rabbit's pocket watch. Ava found a "hobbit hole" on the Library grounds. Even though Davey had visited the Library his whole life, he'd never seen this place. The look on Ava's face when he asked what a hobbit hole was made him make a mental note to read about hobbits as soon as he could.

Ava said people rarely visited the hobbit hole because it was well hidden, and she had plenty of time to explore because she wasn't in school right now. Davey thought her comment about school was funny because he didn't feel like he was in school either. Homework never took up much time. Teachers had stopped calling on him. He could breathe here, with her, which was weird considering all her problems. She was the weirdest girl ever. Did that make him weird? He didn't want to think about it. He just knew how he felt.

Ava gave him a rhyme to learn the way to the hobbit hole.

"Can't you just show me the way?" he'd asked.

Her face had fallen. "But you like treasure hunts. I thought this would be...fun?"

She'd said the word like she wasn't sure if she was using it right.

Davey had grinned. "Okay."

As he neared the Library steps and the clock tower boomed behind him, he struggled to remember Ava's rhyme.

> *Look under the stairs but over the hedge;*
> *you'll know you're there when you want to pledge;*
> *walk seven stones, then turn toward the limes;*
> *walk down twelve steps and knock six times.*

She'd told him the stairs were the big monster-guarded stone ones outside the Library, but as Davey reached the steps, he had a moment of doubt. No hedges, no pledges, no stones.

Maneuvering around running kids and tourists, he made his way to the other side of the steps. Concrete stretched above him here, too. He craned his neck, backing up to watch people trudge to the top of the stairs.

That's when he saw the American flag, flapping in the wind.

He must have seen it before, but then again, he'd never had cause to look at the stairs from this angle.

... you'll know you're there when you want to pledge...

The flag stood a couple of hundred feet behind the stairs, he guessed. Davey set off toward it, passing what looked like a bunch of offices beneath the main floor of the Library. Inside these offices, behind large windows, people typed, wrote, read, or fixed books. The books must have been really old because people handled them with gloves. One woman with long, silver hair spilling over her shoulders stared at the page with her lips parted, her eyes wide, a look Davey could only compare to something he'd seen in church.

He reached the flagpole and looked around. The sidewalk ended right behind the flagpole. Lush grass appeared—and so did a hedge. To the right, the hedge stretched and disappeared behind the Library. To the left, it led to a walled-off area. Curious, he followed it to the left until he reached the walls.

One of the walls contained a door of rough, dark wood. A large golden key stuck out from the keyhole. A little note tied with a string to the key read, in tiny cursive, *Please return me to the keyhole when you are done.* Davey turned the key. There was no doorknob, so he pushed the door open.

To his surprise, the walls had no ceiling: The wind ruffled his hair, and he looked up at the sky. Roses vined up and around all four walls made of giant stones that looked almost white. Flowers of all colors ran along the base of each wall, and rings of flowers dotted the grass. When he stepped around the door, thick grass rolled up to a tree with oversized green leaves, the roses from the wall stretching and clinging to it, forming a rose arch. He couldn't believe how many things were blooming in October.

But what drew his attention the most were large, flat stones arcing in three directions: to the center and to the right and left corners. He could easily count seven forward, seven on each side.

Walk seven stones, then turn toward the limes...

The center stones led to a gray fountain with floating lily pads, so he could rule out that path. He stuffed the key in his pocket and walked on the left seven stones. He looked up and grinned: Dark green limes hid under dense leaves.

But he faced a wall. Where was he supposed to turn? He pivoted left to climbing roses. When he turned right, something pulled his attention to the ground.

He blinked. What had looked like a shadow was actually a hole beside the wall, a neat rectangle. Davey edged toward the rectangle and looked down onto carved earth steps in the hole. The stairs curved slightly but so steeply Davey couldn't see the bottom.

Walk down twelve steps and knock six times.

He leaned back as he gingerly placed his foot on the first step, resisting the urge to use them more like a ladder. Despite the colder air and darkness as he descended, he enjoyed the dirt smell. As he counted step six, a light appeared ahead, and by the twelfth, Davey stood at a round wooden door just his height with a doorknob smack in the middle. Another pretend candle—this one in a glass prism—swung above the door. Davey examined the trapped candle, fascinated. *Cool.*

He raised his right hand and rapped six times. The door flew open on the sixth rap.

"Where WERE you? You took forever!" Ava's voice rang high and strained, but he could only make out her shadow.

Davey squinted at the outline of Ava's hair sticking out in all directions. As his sight adjusted, her outline resolved into a mass of red curls, her freckles standing out much more than normal against her paler-than-ever skin. She wore her usual man's shirt and pants that were too small for her. The wrinkles around her forehead and eyes and her fast breathing made him rear back a little, but Ava grabbed him and pulled him inside.

The room was small and cozy, a little larger than his bedroom, with two overstuffed leather chairs and a lamp between them and small tables on either side of the chairs. Ava's backpack leaned against one side table, and a tea set sat on the other. The walls to the right were lined with pegs, one of which held a dark green cloak. To the left was a tiny, unlit fireplace with what looked like real logs. Paintings of shelves lined with books and cabinets covered the walls, punctuated by the image of another arched hallway leading to something resembling a kitchen. The biggest difference was the low ceiling, like it was a place made for kids.

Ava waved her hand at the room. "It's only the sitting room, but I still like it." She exhaled. "I can't wait any longer. I'm not sure how much time we have!"

Davey found his voice. "What? What happened?"

Ava hurriedly explained the lie she told about Ms. Goode and her fear that her father would reach her before she did.

"She's not at the Library yet, but I had this dream—" Ava stopped and bit her lip.

Davey nodded at her to go on.

"I... I—" Ava stuttered, reddening. "I've had this dream over and over. I mean, my whole life."

Davey read the fear on her face. They each took a seat in the big leather chairs, which, Davey found, weren't so big when you sat in them. They fit Davey and Ava just right.

"Ava, you don't have to tell me anything you don't want to." Part of him was also a bit afraid of what she might have to say.

She did a double take. "What did you call me?"

Heat rose in Davey's face. "It's from something I read." He searched her face. "Is that okay? Are you mad? Or worried it might...mess up your cure?"

Tears welled in her eyes, and Davey's stomach clenched with anxiety.

"Davey, I'm not sure of anything anymore. It's...it's a lovely name." She paused. "Please, just...don't call me that except when we're in private, okay?"

"I won't," Davey said, nodding solemnly, his stomach relaxing.

"It's a lovely name," she repeated in a soft voice, looking at her hands clasped tightly in her lap. "I wonder what it's like to be her."

Davey cocked his head to one side, but then Ava continued.

"In the dream," she began, "I'm outside, standing on something. I'm hungry and...dirty. I'm so hungry I could faint. There's...a crowd around me."

"Like an audience? You were in a play?"

"No, there's...just a few trees around, but mostly I see people and this man on a horse in the distance. And that's when I realize I'm not...me."

"Huh?"

"I reach out to point at this man on the horse..." Ava held up her arm, and Davey's gaze followed her pointing finger to the round door. "And that's when I know I'm not me. It's an...adult arm. It's really thin and dirty."

"You're...dreaming someone else's dreams?"

Ava dropped her arm, and the wrinkles popped up on her forehead again. "I don't know! But...last night...last night was the first time something new happened in the dream."

Davey leaned toward her.

"Last night, I saw a...a pattern...on my...I mean, the woman's...arm."

Davey's eyes widened. "A tattoo?"

"No, the word in my...or her...head was...*brand*."

"But only cattle get brands...I think." Davey chewed his lip in thought. "Yeah. Cows and stuff."

Ava unclasped her hands and held her palms up before letting them drop into her lap. "It's just what I dreamt. And I drew something...after."

"Oh yeah? You drew the brand, you mean?"

Ava grimaced. "No...these...don't make sense. Look, I brought them." She unzipped her backpack and slid off the chair to hand the sheaf of papers to Davey.

"Whoa." He had to accept them with both hands. He picked up one, turned it over, then another. "How long were you drawing? These have drawings on both sides."

"Hours. I don't know if I've ever drawn so long." She paused. "They're like...shadows to me."

Davey flipped through them, frowning. "Oh yeah, I see what you mean. Just like...different shades of...weird shapes and stuff I don't recognize." He looked up at her and put them on the side table.

She met his gaze. "I don't get it either. Usually I'd give these to Father to burn, but...I didn't."

Davey nodded. "I don't blame you." He paused. "Um, how do you feel about doing that—keeping them?"

Ava didn't answer right away. Then she uncrossed her arms and rested her hands on her stomach. "My stomach hurts when I think about *him*."

Davey's shoulders sagged a little.

Ava went on. "But when I think about the *drawings*...and I hold them..." She glanced at Davey and, to his shock, a small smile played on her lips. The wrinkles left her forehead. "I don't know why, but it feels right. I feel bad when I think about Father, but...it feels right in my heart to keep these, Davey."

Davey exhaled slowly, thinking of the conversation with his ma.

She frowned. "But I wish I could show you the brand. I think it's important. I'm not sure why..."

"Why can't you draw it for me now?"

Ava slid off the chair and took a step back, wrapping her arms protectively around herself again. "You know why. Look what happened to Johnny. And there were others, Davey. In the boxes in the basement." She averted her gaze.

"But the brand is a thing. And I didn't see any people in those," Davey said, jerking his thumb toward the pile of sketches behind him. "Are you afraid someone's gonna get hurt because of those?"

Ava looked at the sketches, shook her head. "They're...different. But Davey, I still didn't choose to draw them. It just happened. Like always."

"Ava, a brand isn't a person, so you can't hurt anybody." He stood up, put the drawings on his chair, and took her hand. It trembled in his. "I think you need to try to draw what you saw in your dream. *Because* you want to."

Ava pulled her hand away with a shuddering gasp.

"I don't WANT to!" Ava shouted, eyes bulging with tears.

Davey stepped back, stuffed his hands in his pockets.

"How come?" he asked, his lips pressed tight, avoiding her eyes because he was half nervous and half angry.

Ava paced the small room. "I don't want to do anything that could mess up the cure, Davey, if there's a chance a cure still exists. And Father said I had to do everything he said, exactly..." She stopped pacing and stole a glance at Davey.

"He told you not to draw?" Davey asked.

"I only do it if I can't help it, which hasn't happened in a long time except for these shadow drawings and"—she shivered—"Johnny. And when he asks me to draw. Otherwise, it's too dangerous."

Davey held up a hand. "Wait. Stop. When does he ask you to draw?"

Ava's eyes darted nervously around the small room, and she retreated behind her chair. "When he says...it's necessary."

"Do you draw...people?"

Ava's fingers dug into the ruddy-colored leather and she nodded.

"Like...who?"

"The people who come to his church...his congregants, I mean. People in town..."

"Congregants? Yeah, I thought he reminded me of a preacher."

"Reverend," Ava corrected. "They call him Reverend Mather."

He cocked his head to one side. "Why would you need to draw anybody for him?"

"When he needs something," Ava struggled, "he puts his hands on my shoulders, and my eyes are closed, and he tells me a story that ends with a question. I...kind of draw the answer." Ava swallowed. "But it's always about people."

"He asks a question, and you draw the answer," Davey repeated.

"After the story. Like I've said before, I don't know what the answer is, it just...comes out on the paper."

"What's the story about?" Davey asked.

Ava fell silent for a while. "They're sad stories. I never, I mean, no one's asked me before, so I hadn't thought about it. I can't draw unless I...feel something."

"So...he won't allow you to draw because you want to, but he gets you to draw...because *he* wants you to."

Ava covered her eyes with her palms.

"It's just," Davey said softly, "you still want to follow his rules, but you said you weren't sure you could trust him."

She lowered her hands, and tears streamed down her face. "But he's...all I...have!"

With a mix of a growl and a scream, she scrambled forward. Davey flattened himself against the wall. Ava snatched up her drawings and flung them across the room. For a brief moment, it rained sketches.

Ava covered her face and sobbed. "I'm sorry! I don't know what to believe, I don't know what's real!"

Davey's face crumpled. He went to Ava's side, their shoulders almost touching.

"He's not all you have." He jammed his hands back into his pockets. "It just feels like it." His heart gave a dull, sickening thud with the hole his own dad had left.

Ava slowly dropped her hands from her face and threw her arms around his neck. Stunned, Davey stiffened and played statue until it ended.

Ava touched her nose with the sleeve of her oversized shirt. She turned to take in the rest of the room. "I made such a mess."

They both stared at the papers scattered across the floor, some sliding down a curved wall, others halfway under the door.

"This is closer to how I used Punchy the Clown," Davey observed.

"Poor Punchy."

They didn't look at each other, but Ava snorted, and that made Davey laugh.

"Ava, I didn't mean to try to force you, you know, to do anything."

Now Ava's hand slipped into his and gave his hand a gentle squeeze. Davey flushed but he squeezed her hand back.

Slowly his eyes widened, and he yanked his hand away.

"Ow, Ava, what gives? You're squeezing me so hard that—" Davey stopped as Ava pointed at something on the floor.

"Do you see it?" she whispered.

"What?" he whispered back.

"The hand."

"A hand! Where?" Davey's head pivoted around the room, his face wild. He jumped when Ava touched his shoulder.

"No, the hand...or, I mean, you can see part of the arm and the beginning of the hand." Ava hopscotched around her drawings until she reached a cluster near the door. She nudged four shadow drawings closer together. "Now do you see it? Like a hand pointing? Or part of one?"

"Uh, maybe?" Davey squinted at it. "But that shape...could be lots of things."

Ava pursed her lips and surveyed the carpet of drawings around her. "You're right...but it looks so...familiar." She bent over, straining her eyes, then stood.

"It's so dark in here, Davey."

"Hey!" Davey perked up. "We can go up to the garden. Everything was dry, and it has a wall and"—he pulled the key out of his pocket and held it up—"no one will bug us."

Ava grinned, and Davey helped her pick up the drawings around the room. She produced a heavy silver key from her backpack and locked the round door behind them, standing on tiptoe to slide the key on top of the door behind the light.

They took the earth stairs up through the hole and found themselves blinking when they encountered real sunlight at the top.

Ava dropped her backpack right at the mouth of the hole, gathered the drawings, and hurried to the garden gate. She held the drawings to her chest for a moment, then walked to the far left of the wall and began laying them out, one by one. Sometimes she stopped, flipped a drawing over, then continued.

Davey stood awkwardly near the hole, but when the wind picked up and rustled some of the pages, he gathered a handful of the small black and white stones that framed the rings of flowers. He quickly caught up to Ava, placing a stone in the center of each page.

When they finished, they stood near the fountain to take in their work. Ava had made even rows of the sketches, and they covered half of the walled garden. She walked slowly to the lower right corner and removed one drawing, then walked to the top row and replaced the fifth drawing in with that one. She held the drawing she'd just replaced in her hand and looked around.

"A puzzle," Davey whispered and itched to help her, but he couldn't see at all how they worked together. They looked like random shapes to him, but Ava seemed to sense how they fit. He didn't want to slow her down, so he found a small bench. He sat watching Ava until the sunlight had tilted the shadows. Ma would wonder where he was...

"I finished."

Davey peered up at Ava, her hair a candy-apple silhouette in the late afternoon light.

She swallowed and blinked nervously. "I did draw the brand, Davey. Look."

Davey shook himself fully awake and trotted just a short distance behind Ava, around the sketches to the side of the wall with the underground entrance. They both turned around.

It was like looking into a giant, multi-paned window, each stone fixing one pane to the next. But the sight froze his heart, and he wanted to look away.

A single right arm, shriveled to the bone, stretched out from the lower left corner of the window. A faint geometric pattern lay in wrinkled folds on the upper part of the arm. Davey could make out something like circles inside a triangle.

A sea of faces surrounded the arm, men and women, adults and kids. Some looked scared, but most looked excited. Only one person's head turned away to see where she was pointing.

The arm pointed to a figure on horseback who rode on top of a nearby hill directly behind the crowd of people. The figure wore black clothes, had long curly hair spilling over the shoulders, and Davey had the strange sense that the person was smiling even though he couldn't make out the details of the face. And with the coat that stopped at the knee, he could tell it was a man. A man from a long time ago.

He tore himself away to look at Ava, who stared at the window of her drawings as well.

"Have you figured out why her brand is important?" Davey asked.

"It's just...familiar, somehow." She looked at Davey. "Why do I keep dreaming this?"

"I dunno, but I bet you'll keep on dreaming it 'til we figure it out." His eyes slid toward the drawing again, particularly the man on horseback. "And it seems really important that she's pointing at that guy there. Do you know who it is?"

Ava shook her head. "But," she added, "I did draw something on the other side..."

"Oh yeah!" Davey's eyes widened with excitement, but then he raised his head to the fading sun and his tone filled with disappointment. "I'm sorry, Ava, but I should get back. I usually don't stay this long, and Ma will worry. Can we—"

But then he fell silent when they heard a scuffling sound just outside the garden walls. They exchanged worried looks, but Davey took a deep breath, ran to the gate, and flung it open.

Out of the corner of his eye, he could've sworn he saw the flap of black robes disappearing around the hedge. His nostrils flared.

A faint scent of smoke still hung in the air.

CHAPTER 11—EVIL

3 days until the Anniversary

After Davey left, Evil gathered her drawings, scattered the stones with the others, and replaced the gold key in the garden door. She ran straight to the front desk area on the main floor. She had to find Ms. Goode to explain that she'd lied to her father about her because...because why? She wasn't sure how much she could say except it was to protect herself and that she was sorry.

An older woman with piles of curls on top of her head turned away abruptly when Evil caught her staring. Barton, one of the older teenagers who worked there random nights and weekends, had multiple binders spread out on one of the desks behind the staff area.

"Excuse me!" Evil whispered loudly, but Barton didn't look up. "Barton!"

Barton wrote slowly and carefully in a binder.

Evil whisper-barked, "BARTON!" This time he raised his eyes to hers in surprise, looked left and right, then slowly pushed back from the desk. Evil shifted her feet in anticipation as he made his way to her.

"Hey...uh, you. You need help or something?" He looked like he really wanted her to say no.

"Did Ms. Goode come in yet?"

He looked away. "Uh, yeah, she did."

Evil exhaled with relief. "May I talk to her?"

"Actually, uh, she's... Well, your dad's talking to her. In one of the empty meeting rooms, since Sundays are slow." He tilted his head in the direction of the rooms.

"Thank you!" Evil said as she fled around the desk. Small glassed-in meeting rooms lined the back wall. Many rooms were dark, but finally she spotted her father and Ms. Goode, both of them standing in the middle of a room. They looked like a pair of mourners, her father in his black robes, Ms. Goode in a cropped black jacket and flared black pants, an oversized velvety-looking bag on the table. The librarian's arms were folded, her face serious, and her father kept alternately touching the crest around his neck, then making strange motions like he was rolling the air around in his hands as he spoke to her.

Why weren't they sitting at the table? But then she saw her father's hands fly up into the air as his mouth widened and his lips moved faster, and she guessed why.

She stopped. What was she thinking? What would she say, bursting into the room? Evil stepped back until she assumed she was out of their view, then made a beeline for the room next to them. She ducked in, took off her backpack, and slid down the wall. She kept the light off as she leaned her head back and angled her right ear to the wall.

She couldn't hear Ms. Goode's murmured responses, but a sharp puff of air told Evil she was using her inhaler. That's when her father raised his voice.

"...stay AWAY from my child and FIND the boxes, and perhaps you'll get to keep your JOB, Ms. Goode!"

Evil's eyes widened and her mouth trembled. She closed her eyes in concentration, but she couldn't understand what Ms. Goode said in response. Had he called Ms. Goode a liar when she said she didn't know what he was talking about? Had she accused HIM of lying? Evil's heart raced. What had she done?

As these thoughts swirled in Evil's head, her father exited the room. His robes flew behind him as he rounded the corner.

Ms. Goode soon followed. Her long braid swung behind her as she passed Evil in the opposite direction her father had taken. Panic overtook Evil. She had to say something to her—but what? Just as Ms.

Goode rounded the opposite corner, Evil stood up and decided that most of all, she had to apologize for what had happened. Then she'd try to stick as close to the truth as she could. It didn't make it okay, but she had to do...something.

Evil followed swiftly in Ms. Goode's path, but when she reached the corner and peered toward the main desk, no Ms. Goode. Barton looked up briefly, but when he caught Evil's eye, he looked down again and hunched over his binders. Evil's eyes rose toward the main staircase, but she saw only strangers. She then fast-walked to the hallways.

At the end of the first hall, Evil caught Ms. Goode disappearing behind one of the doors marked Under Construction after fastening a large ring of keys to her belt. Evil looked around and then ran to the door, shocked when it actually opened. She slipped inside as quietly as she could, then counted how many steps she heard Ms. Goode take as her eyes adjusted to the lighting of the small electric candles.

At twenty-eight steps, the footsteps stopped. Next, keys jangled, a loud click echoed against the stone, and a door creaked open and shut.

Evil treaded softly up the steps, counting to match Ms. Goode's path. When she reached the fifth landing, she stood at a dark wooden door with a small brass label that read *The Plath Room*.

Her stomach curdled. Was Ms. Goode crying? Would she yell at Evil for lying? Worse, tell her father? Evil closed her eyes and forced herself to knock twice.

A muffled "Come in, Barton," came from within the room.

Evil winced and bit her lip but said nothing. She breathed in and out again before she turned the iron door handle.

She blinked at the darkness that greeted her. Silver points of light dotted curving walls, and a long couch stretched out to her right. To the left, toward the middle of the room, a figure sat at a small table. Glass clinked, and the figure stood. As Evil's eyes adjusted, a teacup and saucer resolved themselves on top of a small round table, and the figure became the librarian, Ms. Goode. The librarian's lips parted as she looked at Evil.

Evil still held the iron handle and gripped it harder, wanting to run, trying not to.

"Come in," Ms. Goode called to her in a soft voice. "But please close the door."

Evil closed the door, then stood there, wary and uncertain.

Ms. Goode closed the gap between them. Evil tensed, but warmth flowed through her like she'd stepped into a bath. It felt so soothing Evil suddenly wanted to cry.

"I'm...Reverend Mather's daughter. I... I'm so sorry, Ms. Goode. I lied, I lied to my father about you," she sputtered, but to her surprise, Ms. Goode put her finger to her lips and shook her head. Evil stopped talking.

"While normally I wouldn't approve of lying," she said in a quiet, deep voice, "these are trying times."

Evil furrowed her brow, puzzled.

"I never let on it was a lie," the librarian continued. "He thought I was going to prevent him from using the kiln in the basement."

"Kiln?" Evil repeated, mystified at what she was hearing.

"It's how you fire the clay." Ms. Goode closed her eyes for an extra-long blink. "In this case, your lie has helped us. Given us another clue to what he's up to."

Us? Clue? Evil blinked and scrunched up her face. *What was she talking about?*

The librarian took a step back and clasped her hands. Evil craned her neck to look up at her.

"We've been waiting for you for such a long, long time," said Ms. Goode.

CHAPTER 12—EVIL

3 days until the Anniversary

What Ms. Goode said surprised Evil so much that she stared at the librarian in silence for some time.

"You...knew I was following you?" she finally stammered, confused by what the librarian had said about waiting.

Ms. Goode smiled with kind, tearful eyes. "No, I didn't know. In fact, what I just said was probably very confusing, and I shouldn't have said it. I'd like to explain." She gestured to the table. Evil followed her and sat down at the only other chair, taking her backpack off and tucking it under the table. Ms. Goode picked it up.

"We can keep it right over here beside the cabinet. Okay?"

The librarian tucked the backpack on the hidden side of the cabinet, where Evil could just make out a strap of her backpack. The librarian bent down and produced a second teacup and saucer from the cabinet, as well as a small plate, and set it all before Evil. She poured something hot from a thermos and pulled out a small package from her misshapen bag on the bench beside her.

"This is cream tea," the librarian said, "and it goes very well with some biscuits."

Ms. Goode removed two flat, hard "biscuits" from the package and placed them on Evil's plate. The biscuits looked like large crackers to Evil, but when she bit into one, it tasted like a cookie.

Evil sipped the tea, and the warmth spread through her chest. "It's good."

"I thought you would like it. I make my tea very sweet. Let me get some extra sugar, though, just in case."

Evil sipped some more, her eyes wandering around the room as Ms. Goode fussed in the nearby cabinet. Frameless drawings outlined in silver splashed across the walls, sweeping around the half-moon-shaped room: a woman's shoes, a profile of a man with shaggy hair, and then an archway surrounded by cracked walls, leading to more and more archways winding their way through what must surely be an old city. Evil wanted to walk through it...

"We thought she would like this room."

Jarred from her imagination, Evil looked up at the librarian.

"Who?"

"Sylvia Plath. You're far too young to read her, but we hope you'll read her, someday."

"Why do you keep saying 'we'?" Normally Evil would consider asking a question like that rude, but to her surprise, Ms. Goode made her feel like she could ask anything. She didn't act like most adults, who typically avoided Evil or talked down to her.

"My...senior colleagues, here at the Library. We form the Board that makes all the major decisions. I also act as Director so that I can be actively involved in Library acquisitions and maintenance on a regular basis." The librarian topped off Evil's tea from her thermos and sat down. "I replaced my mother as Director some years ago." Her big eyes lowered to her teacup as she spoke.

Evil licked the crumbs off of her lips. "Did you find my great-great-great-grandfather's diary?"

"No. It found the Library, really, thanks to an anonymous sender. The Community did fashion the Library in a way that we thought might lure it here one day, though."

"Lure?"

"Yes. They—the founders, the Community—believed that all books would want to live here."

Evil bit into another biscuit. *I like living here.*

"I can't believe the day has finally come." She looked at Evil, her eyes brimming and sad, but her mouth turned up and happy. "Have you ever cried out of happiness?"

Evil shook her head, stunned.

"I think someday you will...Ava."

All the air left Evil's lungs. "How...how do you know...that name?"

The librarian's face lit up. "I wasn't sure how you would react when I called you that. The sound of a boy calling that name has come to me several times at the Library, coupled with a picture of you in my mind. It's quite unbidden. I've actually turned around to see who's whispering behind me, but no one ever is. I saw you in my mind, briefly, and then you vanished. But I was left with this feeling that this name was yours."

Frightened by how much Ms. Goode knew and wondering why she was so interested in her, Evil glanced behind her at the door. The librarian noticed.

"I am not holding you here, Ava." The dark circles underneath her even darker eyes suddenly stood out. "You can go at any time. But I think you would be interested in what I have to say." Ms. Goode leaned forward. "Ava, we are here to help."

Evil shrank back against her chair. "Help with what?" she whispered.

"We're here to help you understand who you really are."

Evil stood up so fast her chair fell over.

"I know who I am. I've known my whole life," she replied softly.

Ms. Goode stood up too, her face creased with worry. "I'm so sorry, I just didn't know when...or if...any of us would ever meet you. I don't know if there is an easy way to say any of this, and it's so much, so much to handle for someone your age." She clasped her hands together. "But we're running out of time with the Anniversary just days away and your father expecting the diary..."

The Anniversary, she mentioned it! Why did I come into this room? I can't remember...I can't remember...!

"You know me...you know about the Anniversary..." Evil echoed, backing toward the door as the room seemed to grow dimmer, and the silvery drawings wavered.

The librarian squeezed her eyes shut and waved her hands like she wanted to erase what she just said. "Let me start with something much, much simpler. I want you to trust me." She started toward Evil, but Evil bolted for the door and Ms. Goode stopped. *My backpack. I don't have it.*

The librarian held up a hand. "Ava. Please." She took a deep breath, and her eyes appeared to grow even bigger. "I knew your mother." She placed her hand against her chest. "I'm your aunt."

Evil went rigid, hairs rising on her arms. *No. I'm not supposed to ask about Mother.*

Breathless, Evil managed to say, "Mother doesn't exist. You're lying."

She had to leave. Now.

She dashed around the opposite side of the table to snatch up her backpack and circled back to fling open the door. Ms. Goode never moved.

Evil ran down the stairs, tripping and falling at one point, catching herself but cutting her knee on the landing.

Ms. Goode did not try to follow her.

Evil limped into their living quarters, and her father sat at the table, both plates full of food, the candles burnt quite low. Evil tensed.

Late. I'm late.

He folded his arms. "Did you leave the Library without my permission?"

She shook her head.

"Were you drawing without my permission?"

She shook her head again, but thinking of the shadow drawings in her backpack made her pause. He caught her hesitation.

"Give me your backpack, Evil."

"No." The words were out of her mouth before she could stop them. Both she and her father exchanged stunned expressions. He pushed back his chair.

"What did you just say?"

Evil backed away, mute, until she leaned against the wall.

"You'd put everything you've waited your whole life for at risk...now? At the final hour? The Anniversary is almost upon us!"

He stood up and walked over to her, holding out his hand. "I won't let you ruin your life. Give me your backpack."

Evil felt quite certain that if she ran right now, her father would catch her. Then her heart slowed. *But if he takes them away, I might draw them again. I'll keep dreaming about it.*

She slowly held out her backpack to him and wondered why it felt strange.

He unzipped it and looked inside. "Ah. I see you were resenting that I doubted your sincerity." His face softened. "I'm upset that you're tardy and probably letting my own emotions get the best of me. Do you at least have an explanation?"

The Reverend returned her backpack, and she accepted it with both hands, looking inside at the empty shell.

Empty. Empty.

Her mouth completely dry, she collapsed into a dining room chair. "I fell," she rasped. "I...was running on the stairs...like you told me not to...and I fell." She pointed to her bleeding knee.

Her father's eyebrows shot up. "You stay there, Evil. I have some medicine, not to worry." He patted her good knee, then left the room.

Evil dug her nails into her palm as she stared at her backpack. She should never have followed Ms. Goode. She should never have gone into that room.

Ms. Goode stole my sketches.

Later that night, after midnight according to the clock tower, Evil sat up in bed, her arms wrapped around her legs, her teeth chattering, but she wasn't cold. She had turned the lights out so she didn't have to see her drawings, but her eyes were wide open and boring into the darkness. Strange shapes danced in the dark like they always did, and she squinted and begged them to form an answer to her problems. But they only morphed into her father giving a sermon or Ms. Goode running away with her drawings in her arms.

Evil glanced at the shape of her backpack in the corner. She needed answers. Father got her to draw answers when he found it "necessary." When they were at the hobbit hole, Davey said she should draw just because *she* wanted to. But did that mean he thought she could use her drawings to answer her problems like her father did?

Evil shuddered, goosebumps erupting on her legs and arms. What her father found "necessary" was most often about his congregants or other locals back home. And on the Anniversary, he always made time for her drawing after everyone left. Their own small Anniversary. She covered her eyes, remembering.

After they recited the history of the Mathers and witches on that Anniversary, his hands rested lightly on her shoulders. Evil sat at their dining room table back in Boston, hands poised with pencils over her sketch pad. A small picture of Leila Bishop, the mother of one of her classmates, sat in front of her, a small candle lit on either side of it.

"Leila Bishop refuses to attend our church and beats her children, Evil. Beats them. Have I ever beaten you?" Her father spoke in his sermon voice.

Evil shook her head fiercely.

"That is why that little girl in your class has the mark on her cheek. It's from her mother's hand." He paused, but Evil's hands did not move.

"She locks this girl in the closet," he continued. "The girl throws herself against the walls because she is so afraid."

Evil gasped and her hands twitched.

"Yes, she's afraid of the dark, and her mother ignores her screams. That's why she rarely talks at school—she's lost her voice from so much screaming and crying in the dark, dark closet. We could help her children if we had the means."

A single tear ran down Evil's cheek, and her eyes fluttered closed.

Her father's voice got deeper. "This is critical, Evil. It's for our family as much as hers." He paused. "How, Evil, how can we get Leila Bishop to donate her recent inheritance to our church?"

And Evil's hands began to move across the page.

When she opened her eyes, a sketch of an oil slick on a nearby mountainous road sat before her. As usual, she didn't know what it meant. But Leila Bishop's car careened into the mountainside that same night. As she lay dying in the hospital, she changed her will without explanation. Her inheritance would now go to the Mather church.

Evil only found this out from hiding in the school bathroom during recess. Most kids avoided her, but that day they shot her dirty looks. When she cried to her father later that day, frightened that she'd done something terrible, he patted her hair and let her weep into his robes.

"I am merely putting your Curse to the best possible use, Evil. She's been redeemed."

"But she DIED!" Evil wailed into his robes.

"As all of us will," he said, rubbing her back. "As all of us will."

He gently pulled her from his shoulder to look at him.

"I only do what's best, Evil. For you. For us. For my congregants. Doing what's right can be painful, but that is our lot in life as Mathers. We do what's *right*, no matter how painful."

She didn't understand, though, and late that night, a nightmare jarred her out of sleep. She opened her bedroom door to get a drink of water, but the light under her father's study door caught her eye. It felt awfully late for her father to still be awake. She tiptoed to the door and pressed her ear against it.

"Yes, it's done," he murmured inside. "You can cross her off the list, but we can assess the children later." He sighed. "Of course I'm well aware that it's still happening, but does that mean we should cease in our mission? I think not." Then he growled into the receiver, "I'm doing my very best to control the situation until we find a solution. Then we can end this once and for all, I'm sure of it."

Fresh tears sprang to Evil's eyes. As usual, her father was working to find a cure for the Curse.

Reliving this memory, Evil's stomach lurched. What did it all mean now?

Even if he lied about her drawings, he was only using them to do what was best. Wasn't he? Her heart thudded as she struggled with these thoughts that grew long, twisted and vined, weaving in and out, making knots, growing thorns, hiding the girl beneath...

What is real? What is real?

She squeezed her eyes until spots bloomed under her lids, forcing her mind to stop racing in circles. She took slow, deep breaths and looked at her backpack again. She shook her head. She wasn't ready to try to draw on her own, just because she wanted to.

So where did that leave her—searching for where Ms. Goode hid her drawings? And what if Ms. Goode figured out how they went together and saw what Evil had dreamt...what would she think then?

She rubbed her eyes, tired and anxious at the same time at the thought. She might as well look, maybe find out where Ms. Goode had an office and say she left something there? Ask to be let in? Evil frowned, the lie tasting sour. She didn't want to get used to being a liar.

But she had to get up. She wasn't going to sleep anytime soon. And her father had said he was going to be sculpting tonight, quite late, so she probably didn't need to even worry about sneaking away.

Sure enough, after Evil had painfully pulled on some jeans she'd outgrown years ago and an oversized old shirt of her father's, she peeked outside her bedroom: Her father's door stood ajar. He always closed it when she slept. Relieved, she walked down the hallway and let herself out of their quarters and into the Library passageway.

Something crinkled under her foot and she leapt away, looking down.

One of her shadow drawings stared up at her. Her lip trembled.

She snatched it up and held it protectively. Another piece of paper sat at the very end of the hall. Evil ran toward it.

Please don't, please don't say it's my drawing—my father might have seen it, please...

But it was another shadow drawing.

Hands shaking, she grabbed this one too, now turning her head frantically to make sure there weren't any more.

Another paper fluttered to her left, no more than fifteen feet away. Evil glanced around and gave quick thanks that the Library didn't have many visitors that night. She flew to the next paper.

Looking up, a trail of her drawings led around to the next hallway.

Evil raced along, picking them up as fast as she could, her legs quaking with fear.

The trail of drawings led to a stairwell that had no sign about construction or being closed for any reason. Evil looked inside, and more drawings fluttered on the stone stairs.

The trail of drawings led her up one...

Two...

Three...

Four...

Five flights of stairs.

Six, seven, eight, nine, ten, eleven.

Twelve flights of stairs.

The drawings finally stopped at a large, arched wooden door with *The Community Room* etched in fine cursive on the brass plate.

It opened before she could think of what to do next. Evil stood there, holding the mess of papers against her chest, her throat tight, her heart deafening in her ears.

Ms. Goode stood in the doorway, her face serious, her eyes sad.

Evil couldn't find her voice. She couldn't move her legs.

Ms. Goode took off her cropped jacket and tossed it behind her into the room. She squatted in front of Evil in the doorway, and the dark shadows under her huge eyes made Evil step back.

The librarian held out her right arm to Evil, pointing with her left index finger to the upper part of her arm.

"Don't you think we should talk now?"

Evil turned to examine the woman's arm, and her breath escaped in a rush of shock. The drawings fell from her arms.

The brand. Ms. Goode had the brand from her dreams.

CHAPTER 13—EVIL

2 days until the Anniversary

Evil's legs wobbled, and Ms. Goode swiftly stood and steadied her, placing her hands on Evil's shoulders.

"You're branded," Evil whispered, wishing the floor would stop tilting. But as warmth spread from where Ms. Goode's hands touched her shoulders, the floor gradually stilled.

"It's a tattoo," the librarian corrected, "but I wanted to see if you recognized it. I'm sorry to be so dramatic, but with your father wanting the diary by the Anniversary, you have a lot to learn in very little time." She guided Evil's shaky hands to one side of the steady door frame, then began gathering her drawings from the floor.

"How do you know about the Anniversary?" Evil's nails dug into the doorframe.

Ms. Goode did not look up from gathering the drawings. "We had to understand why deaths in the Community would spike every year at a certain time. And your father has asked to see the diary on that very night, though it's not likely to be finished."

"But it has to be…" Evil's voice trailed off as Ms. Goode cast a questioning look at Evil.

Evil looked away, too weak and confused to do anything but cling to the doorframe. "My father might have seen these drawings. Why…?" Her voice trailed off, and she leaned her forehead against the wood.

Ms. Goode's head snapped up. "There's no time for fainting. Let's get you some tea."

Evil continued to grip the doorframe fearfully. The librarian squatted down again.

"Ava, the door will remain unlocked the entire time you are in this room. You can leave at any time. And your father didn't see anything. He's fussing over his clay dolls again." Her face darkened briefly, but then she shook her head as if to rid herself of something. "I thought you'd come looking for your drawings after he left."

Ms. Goode straightened up, the complete set of drawings in her arms. "You don't need to be scared. Did I try to catch you when you left some hours ago?"

Evil shook her head.

"Did I tell your father you were lying when he accused me of talking to you about him?"

Evil shook her head again and her grip relaxed.

Ms. Goode handed the drawings back to Evil, who finally released her hold on the frame and accepted them with surprise.

"I never intended to keep your drawings. It was just a desperate move on my part, some insurance against you panicking and leaving, which you did, and which is understandable."

The librarian stepped inside the room.

"Now you can decide. You can come in and hear what I have to say, and I won't stop you if you try to leave at any point. Or you can turn away from me."

Evil blinked, startled at the personal way Ms. Goode had put the choice.

The librarian stood aside as Evil poked her head into the room. Like the other room, it was dark, but this one didn't have any silver drawings on the wall, just some kind of wallpaper, she guessed, squinting. A rough wooden table sat in the center, but that was all she could make out in the glow of the solitary fat candle sitting on the table. It was like a picnic table that hadn't been quite finished, with a long bench on either side. The table held two plates of Ms. Goode's strange biscuits, two cups and saucers, and a large white teapot covered in purple-black roses. The gold rims of the teacups glimmered in the candlelight.

Evil glanced at Ms. Goode and nodded. The librarian turned and walked toward the table as Evil closed the door, then opened it again, testing it. It was not locked.

She laid the pile of drawings beside the door and sat down across from Ms. Goode, who had put on her jacket again. Evil sniffed the air.

"Why does it smell like a farm? I mean," Evil added hastily, "in a good way."

The librarian gave a small laugh. "It's because of the straw."

Evil blinked at the floor, then squinted into the darkness beyond their table. "I don't see any."

"It's mostly in the corners, for effect. I'll put on the central light soon and you'll see."

Evil's stomach rumbled as Ms. Goode poured her tea. The librarian smiled and gestured toward the biscuits. These had chocolate on one side.

"Go on, I have plenty. Sounds like you didn't eat enough for dinner. English biscuits can be quite filling."

Evil stared at her plate, imagining the flaky round shapes of baked bread she knew as biscuits. She picked up what was very clearly a flat vanilla cookie shaped like a fluffy cloud and put it down again.

"Ms. Goode, thank you for the tea and …biscuits. Last time, too."

The librarian's smile faltered as she finished pouring her own tea. "You know, Ms. Goode was my mother. You can call me Julia if you like."

Evil hurriedly finished a bite of cookie-biscuit and swallowed. "Really?" No adult had ever offered their first name for her to use.

The librarian nodded as she sipped her tea. Tiny roses twined around the cup, and the handle formed the green stemmed base. Brown and green vined swirls decorated the saucer.

"Ava," Ms. Goode asked as she carefully set her teacup on the saucer, "why did you call my tattoo a brand?"

While Evil had been anxious the first time the librarian used her Davey-given name, now it put her at ease. Like she was with Davey, but she couldn't say why.

"I've dreamt about it. A lot. I just didn't know until recently that it was a brand. I mean, my dream said it was a brand." Evil twisted in her seat to point to the drawings by the door. "I drew it, too."

Ms. Goode's eyes widened. "I didn't see anything but some kind of misty shapes in those sketches. I actually showed you my tattoo for another reason."

"When you put them together," Evil explained, miming laying the drawings out side by side, "they make a picture. The woman in my dream had your...tattoo." Evil hesitated, but Ms. Goode held her gaze with complete seriousness. She licked her lips and continued.

"It was like I could hear her thoughts, and she called it a brand." Evil searched her memory and added, "I know it hurt. A lot. But she didn't want to let anyone know it did."

"Anyone?" echoed the librarian. "Who else was in your dream?" She raised the teacup to her lips.

"Lots of people. A big crowd, just a little below her. And then there was the man in black on a horse."

Evil jumped as Ms. Goode's cup crashed to the saucer and then bounced and skittered on its side, chips of porcelain flying from the lip as tea splashed across the wooden table. She stood, and in the candlelight, a blush formed on her cheeks.

"I'm so sorry, Ava, did any tea splash you?"

Evil looked down at her shirt, then shook her head, her heart beating fast, and she eyed the librarian warily. "Are my dreams...bad?"

Ms. Goode fetched a small cloth from her velvet bag on the floor and mopped up the tea. She delicately held the handle of the cup as she examined it in the candlelight. "Still useable, if you sip from one side," she said, then exhaled slowly as she sat again and poured herself another cup. "I'd say your dreams are both good and bad."

"How can something be both?" Evil asked, bewildered.

The librarian sipped her tea before continuing. "It's bad in that it sounds like you're dreaming about something horrible that changed both of our lives almost three hundred years ago. It's good, though, in that it shows how connected we are."

"How does that dream connect us?"

"They branded the accused witches. And when they hung them, your great-great-great-grandfather Cotton Mather was rather...infamous for wearing black and riding around on his horse in the background."

Evil put down the cookie-biscuit, her stomach tightening, her throat constricting. *They branded the accused witches.*

"Witches..." Evil exhaled. "I'm dreaming about a witch?" She clenched her teeth to keep them from chattering. "I'm a Mather; I'm not a witch!"

Ms. Goode reached out and touched Evil's hand.

"No, you're not a witch. And neither were any of them. But our common ancestor decided to curse Cotton regardless, and what matters, Ava, is that Cotton believed it. And he convinced his whole family that the curse was real." She looked directly at Evil and squeezed her hand. "And you know your father believes it."

Even though Evil's throat relaxed as warmth radiated from Ms. Goode's hand, she still shook her head, confused and frightened. "But I still don't understand. I'm not a witch. I'm a Mather. Why would I dream about a witch?"

"You might be dreaming about a very special person that you think of as a witch." Ms. Goode's eyes found Evil's. "You might be dreaming of *our* ancestor, Ava. Yours and mine. I tried to explain before—I'm your aunt. You're a Mather, yes, but you're also related to Sarah Goode, one of the accused witches and the one to curse Cotton Mather. Because my sister was your mother."

Mother? Evil tasted the word, and it had no flavor. She'd stopped asking questions long ago. Her father said it hurt too much to talk about her, so for Evil, she had ceased to exist. It was easier to believe there was never a mother.

The librarian withdrew her hand.

"I wish I didn't have to tell you all of this at once. I wish we had met sooner, but I didn't want to"—she hesitated—"force it any sooner than I had to."

The knowledge that she might have witch's blood in her made Evil shake, and she rubbed her arms furiously. *No...no...it can't be...it's bad enough to be cursed...it can't be!*

Her head dropped and she stared at her lap. "If you're telling the truth, that I...that we...are related to a"—she checked herself, looking up at Ms. Goode—"this lady, then I really am evil." Tears pricked at her eyes. "You're going to tell me I'm cursed forever."

The librarian sat down again and folded her hands, her big eyes locking on Evil.

"Ava, I am telling you the truth, but the truth is just the opposite of what you're thinking. You're not evil. You're a gift." With that, Ms. Goode bent toward the large candle and blew it out, and Evil couldn't see anything at all.

CHAPTER 14—EVIL

2 days until the Anniversary

A small gasp escaped from Evil just as a central light embedded in the Community Room ceiling poured out a gentle, yellow beam into the darkness. It softened the shock of revealing that Evil and Ms. Goode sat in a prison cell. A prison within the Library.

The strange, muted light fell on walls of large, gray, misshapen stones. Tiny carvings covered the walls. Straw piled up in the corners, and on one pile sat a thick, rusty chain with a clasp just large enough to fit around someone's ankle. A scream gathered in Evil's throat when she raised her eyes to the tiny window above the straw. A sliver of pale moon peered through the crude, glassless frame, and that's when Evil's panic turned into a question mark.

The window was a painting; the moon was painted too. Evil looked at the central light in the room.

Ms. Goode, who must have flicked on a switch behind her, walked in front of the table, the only piece of furniture Evil could see in the cell.

"It's supposed to simulate moonlight," the librarian said, pointing above them at the yellow light.

"We did our best to recreate what the cells looked like back in the late seventeenth century without terrifying us all. We built this to ensure we'd never forget what our ancestors went through."

Ms. Goode walked to the wall closest to them and pointed at the top to some of the carvings. She gestured for Evil to come and look.

Evil pushed back her chair, and when she got close to the wall, her eyes bulged.

"Someone carved all of those words?" Evil stepped closer and eyed the entire wall. "It covers the wall from top to bottom!" She turned and gasped as she took in the walls around her. "It's...everywhere!"

Ms. Goode looked down with a quiet smile. "We allowed ourselves this drama. It's special wallpaper, one we designed—it only looks like it's carved. The content is from the court records of the trials and later, newspaper accounts—or what passed for newspapers at times—of, ah"—she pursed her lips a moment—"let's say events related to those accused of witchcraft, throughout the past several hundred years. We wanted it to look like someone had carved all of these things into the stone like so many prisoners carved their experiences into cells around the world.

"It all started here." The librarian turned to the wall, so Evil did too. Ms. Goode reached out and pressed a part of the wall, and it gave in under her finger a little like a secret button. The light in the center of the room dimmed, and then a bright little moonlight shaft poured directly onto a portion of the wall in front of them. Evil blinked at the jumble of strange letters that stood taller than all the others, entire paragraphs with no periods or commas but capital letters popping up randomly and then lots and lots of misspelled words. Some she could read, though, and her lips trembled as she did:

Accused.

Bitten.

Blood.

The mark.

Prison.

Witchcraft.

Ms. Goode clasped her hands behind her back. "Tell me what you know about the Salem witch trials."

Evil repeated the familiar refrain her father had taught her:

"The wicked of Salem were drawn to the good
but most of all the purity for which the Mathers stood;

the Mathers smote the witches and righteousness had reigned,
    but not before a witch could cast a curse upon their name."

Ms. Goode lowered her head briefly and closed her eyes. She breathed in and out several times before raising her head again and looking at Evil.

"Do you know why Davey calls you Ava?"

Evil tilted her head to one side, remembering. "Because I remind him of a poem, I think."

"It's also because he sees you differently than your father sees you. Would you agree?"

This hadn't occurred to Evil. She weighed what Ms. Goode had just said for a minute before biting her lip and giving a curt nod.

"So you understand how people can know the same person and come away with very different views of them?"

Evil nodded again.

"Please understand that a lot of people saw the Salem witch trials in a very different way from the Mathers." Ms. Goode moved down the wall and gestured to a list of names. "These twenty-five women and men, who were killed or died in prison, were all accused of witchcraft. An infant was not, but she died in prison anyway." She shook her head. "Even a poor dog was hung."

Evil's insides shook at the thought of all that death.

"Years later," the librarian continued, "they were pardoned by public officials, declared completely innocent."

"But the witnesses! And confessions!" Her head spun with what Ms. Goode was telling her.

"The witnesses only provided spectral evidence. The confessions were under torture." She pointed to the rusty, heavy chain, which Evil didn't want to go near. "Imagine if I turned out the light and locked you in here, chained to the wall, because you wouldn't confess to something." A shadow passed over the librarian's face. "People will say a lot of things under torture."

"But...what's spectral?"

"It means spirit; that is, the evidence was based on things no one could see or prove, like being attacked at night with a pin by someone's spirit or being bitten by someone's spirit. Locals who made such claims about attacks could have easily stuck pins into themselves, bitten themselves."

"But why would they say these things at all?" Evil hunched her shoulders at a chill creeping up her back as more scary words leapt out from the walls.

Hung.

Executed.

Died.

"There are lots of theories, some dealing with the real fear of attacks by the Native Americans, the stress of four years of drought, revenge against disliked neighbors, or to acquire someone's land..."

Evil frowned. None of those things added up to her. Witches were bad. The Mathers had fought them for hundreds of years. Her father had taught her that anyone who had witch's blood was a witch themselves and therefore bad. But now, Ms. Goode was saying *she* had witch's blood? *No...it just couldn't be true...*

"I would say that only the accusers could tell us, but"—Ms. Goode pressed her lips together—"I wonder if even they could say."

"And the Curse...the wi—" Evil caught herself. "The *lady* who cursed Cotton?"

The librarian nodded. "Yes, that happened, though it appears everyone except Cotton Mather was too scared to record the full curse. People think it's in the diary. But there is no evidence she had any dealings with witchcraft, Ava." Then she added, "And of course, no one knows the details of the curse since Cotton's diary was lost so long ago. It's one of the things the Community and Mathers have in common: We have both wanted the diary."

It has the cure...doesn't it?

"But, then, why...?" Evil sputtered. She twisted fistfuls of her hair and pulled until tears formed in her eyes.

"We have no evidence of witchcraft, Ava," Ms. Goode repeated, pleading, "but we have endless evidence that the Mathers *believed* they were cursed." She stretched out both arms, palms up, and turned in a slow circle.

"After this portion of the wall about the trials, what follows are all the accounts of the Mathers hunting down members of the Community. Not in any way that we could prove, but we constantly found clues that a Mather was involved with their deaths. We assume it was their attempt to defeat the curse they believed in so fiercely. It's why so many of our relatives fled across the country, to get away from them, to hide." She looked up. "And then to rebuild."

The librarian offered a small, tired smile to Evil. "The Community founded Virtue and created this Library." She gestured to the ceiling. "It's where they used to live. They couldn't reveal who they were to avoid alerting the Mathers, so they chose to promote their values through a *living* library."

"Living?" Evil repeated.

"Yes. One of our key founders, Mrs. Lockwood, the first to head the Children's Realm, came up with the entire idea. For the opening event of the Library in 1865, she asked the children of the town: 'What does a living story look like?' The children came up with the idea of creating the things they read about, the things you see in our displays and stumble upon in unexpected places. And the fervor for doing so has never died down."

Evil's mouth opened in surprise.

"And, to be honest," Ms. Goode continued, "the idea for the Library was in reaction to the Mathers as well. If they were to cling to the past, we were going to evolve. *Evolutionis Doctrina.*"

"Ee-va-loo-CHO-nus," Evil sounded out, "doc-TREEN-ah." *Evolutionis Doctrina*. Evil felt a secret thrill saying the words like a tiny flame she wanted to protect.

"It means *learning is evolution* in Latin. It's throughout the Library." The librarian smiled. "You're a good mimic, Ava. I'm impressed." She put her hands on her knees so her eyes were level with Evil's. "The Community is composed of the descendants of the accused at Salem. We don't know why the Mathers want the diary, but we want it to understand why we've been so persecuted." She sighed. "And to make sure it never starts again."

The tiny flame that *Evolutionis Doctrina* had sparked now winked out. Evil's chest hurt like she was breathing through a straw. Ms. Goode's face grew blurry.

"Prove it," she said, suddenly holding back tears. Years of her few happy memories crowded around her, all focused on the Anniversary, the one day family came, the one day people filled the house. Even if she couldn't participate, even if no one knew she was there, she loved watching them from her hiding place. The eating, the laughter, the celebration. Now Ms. Goode was telling her how bad it was...how bad the Mathers were.

"This...this whole place is built on stories. This could be just another...story." She bit her lip so hard she tasted blood.

The librarian pointed at her tattoo.

"This looks very familiar, doesn't it? A lot like the Mather crest? It's why I showed it to you."

Evil startled, then slowly nodded, realization spreading over her. That was another reason why she couldn't stop thinking about the brand. It reminded her of something: the Mather crest. Why? She wrapped her arms around herself, hunching her shoulders.

The librarian fished in her velvet bag and emerged with a small pad and a pen. She drew the brand on the piece of paper and held it up for Evil. Embedded circles overlapping a triangle.

"This is the brand. Now watch."

Evil leaned forward. The librarian made a circle around the brand and then slowly drew a large *X* within the circle.

The Mather crest.

It was too much for Evil. Her mind zeroed in on the one last thing she wanted to know.

"But the Curse is real because I'm cursed. I am," she insisted, quietly, as exhaustion gripped her. *My drawings make bad things happen, Ms. Goode.* But Evil couldn't bring herself to say it out loud.

Ms. Goode must have noticed her tiredness because she guided Evil to a chair and sat beside her. "I am so sorry I've had to tell you so much, so fast. It's not fair. But Ava, listen to me: Your father might have raised you to believe you were cursed, *but ever since you were born, the Mathers have stopped their persecution of the Community.* We don't know why. We also don't know why they have been dying at an unusual rate themselves."

Memories bubbled up of counting the arriving Mathers for the Anniversary from her window. Each year there were fewer. *All the accidents since I was born...*

The librarian exhaled sharply. "It's almost like our situations reversed, except we're not trying to kill anyone."

She clasped Evil's hands in hers. "To us, you're not cursed." She smiled, and without meaning to, Evil relaxed like a warm blanket had been wrapped around her shoulders. "You're why we allowed a Mather into the Library at all."

"Me?" Evil mouthed, shocked.

"Yes. If your birth changed the fate of the Community, we could not reject an opportunity to"—Ms. Goode hesitated—"engage you. Since we don't know why the Mathers want it, we need to read the diary before your father gets it."

Evil's head shot up in surprise. "But...you can't! Only a Mather can read the diary!"

"We did hear of an anonymous letter of warning about that in the pocket of the man who died reading the diary." Ms. Goode pressed her lips together. "But I try very hard not to encourage superstition, any more than I would encourage a belief in witchcraft."

"But... how would you get the diary before Father?"

"The antiquarian has explicit instructions to bring the diary only to me the moment he's done. Your father will believe the restoration ran into difficulties and is taking longer than we thought. Due to some concerned members of the Community, we actually have someone else making a replica of the diary for the Library event, just as a precaution, considering its...rather harrowing roots." She shook her head. "Not everyone shares my skepticism of superstition."

"A *replica*?" Evil asked.

"Wood, actually," Ms. Goode pronounced. "It mimics leather well, at a distance. Normally I would abhor fooling the public, but"—she leveled her gaze at Evil—"there is nothing normal about this, to be fair to the concerns of the other Community members."

Evil turned her eyes to the floor.

"Ms. Goode..." She paused, then started again. "Ms. Goode." She looked up at the librarian.

The woman smiled a real smile, a trusting smile, and tilted her head expectantly.

"My father says the diary will lift the Curse, *my* Curse," she whispered. "That once he reads it, and only he can understand it, he'll know how to make me...normal."

The woman's eyes widened. "That's why he wants it?" She touched her tongue to her front teeth briefly and muttered, "Normal...he wants you to be...normal."

Ms. Goode blinked, looked at Evil as if she had just remembered she was there, and raised her chin.

"Ava, if the diary is that important, and given what I've told you...you *absolutely* need to get it first, don't you?"

In the wee hours of the night, Evil pleaded sleepiness to Ms. Goode, still unable to call her "Julia." Though her eyes burned, she didn't want to sleep in her room. She wanted to escape. Her shadow drawings weighed down her backpack, but she feared leaving them behind.

She kept her head down to avoid the few meandering tourists as she hugged the walls. The floor beneath her feet morphed into something that resembled a hard-packed dirt path. Painted trees appeared on the walls around her and grew larger until the hall opened into a spacious room, a fairy forest with a beautiful feast on a table covered in a shiny white tablecloth in the middle.

An enormous photograph of a tunnel of arching trees spread over the back wall, a late-afternoon sun making dappled points of light along the dirt trail. The path beneath her feet continued across the room and through the photograph, beneath the hovering trees. Shaggy green carpet framed the path. On the other walls, dark clusters of painted trees surrounded her as if she'd walked into the heart of a deep forest, and the only way out was to walk into the photograph. The silhouettes of Alice and the Mad Hatter crept amongst the trees.

She dropped her backpack and sat at the tea party table. She gazed over the familiar rubbery tea cakes, finger sandwiches, and cupcakes. The food was all detailed, painted rubber except for one real treat the children were challenged to find. Evil's attention fell to the plate of cupcakes, homing in on the center one with a pale pink rose that reflected the light differently from the others. She carefully nudged the other cupcakes out of the way and lifted the real one. Then she slowly peeled the wrapper off as she tried to make sense of what Ms. Goode had told her.

Evil didn't feel anything when the librarian said they were related or that she knew her mother. She'd never known her mother, never even seen a picture of her. She'd died while having Evil, her father said, and refused to say more. It hurt too much to talk about it, he said. Just one more reason for Evil not to question him, she realized for the first time.

But what mattered to Evil very much was *how* they were related. Ms. Goode claimed she was related to a witch—Evil still couldn't think of them any other way. And not just any witch. Evil stopped eating the cupcake and covered her eyes.

Sarah Goode. Their common ancestor was Sarah Goode, the witch who had cursed the Mathers.

But...

What if Ms. Goode was telling the truth? Had the Mathers really hurt her Community?

Did Ms. Goode think of Evil as part of her Community? Or because she was a Mather, was she not allowed?

Or worse—was Evil an enemy? Was this idea that she was a gift just...a lie?

She'd asked Ms. Goode why she was telling her all of this.

Because you're my niece and you deserve to know who you really are and why you've been raised to think differently.

And if Ms. Goode was telling the truth, then the Mathers had done a lot of very bad things. The Mathers, not the witches...or the accused, as Ms. Goode called them.

Did that mean her father...?

Evil shuddered. No, her father was the Reverend Stanley Mather. Even if he'd lied to Evil about burning her drawings, he helped people.

The forest seemed to grow a little darker. Evil's chest felt heavy.

I'm the one who hurts people.

The Mad Hatter appeared to shake a shadow finger at her. *Your father asked you to draw people—you didn't mean to hurt anyone. He asked you!*

But, Evil argued, he always said it was what was best for the family. It was critical, something she wasn't allowed to question.

Now all Evil had in her head were questions. Questions her father would not answer. Questions she didn't want to ask Ms. Goode.

Evil stared at the cupcake, then sought out Alice in the dense trees on the left-hand wall. Alice peered around a tree, and unlike the Mad Hatter, a little light fell on her face. Evil examined her expression. With her big eyes and firm mouth, she looked confused and fierce all at the same time.

Everything is opposite. Is a reverend bad and a witch good? Can you be both sad and happy? Confused and fierce?

But no matter what was true, everyone wanted to know what was in Cotton's diary.

Ms. Goode believed it would reveal why the Community had been "hunted."

Her father thought it would cure her.

But what did Evil think?

I don't KNOW what to think!

She swung her legs in anger and knocked her backpack on its side. It thudded softly, heavy with the drawings. Her mind latched on to them, her dreams seeming more solid than anything else, since they hardly changed at all.

My dreams are trying to tell me something. Even Ms. Goode thinks so. And I've never drawn on both sides before.

Evil gasped. Both sides. She'd forgotten...they were trying to tell her something, but she hadn't looked at the other side. She had told Davey she'd wait for him, but now panic seized her at the thought of waiting another second.

Evil ate the cupcake in two giant bites, her mind popping with the sugar. She bounded to her feet and looked around.

She was a ball of sweat at the end, but once she'd moved the chairs and inched the table oh-so-slowly to rest against the wall, she finally had enough room.

Evil dumped the drawings out of her backpack and began spreading them out across the carpet and path. She then picked up one drawing. Turned it over. Stared again.

Oh no. I can't tell which side is which.

She found Alice in the trees again. Now she understood that look.

Evil's eyes itched and her limbs ached when she was done. Her stomach growled. She wasn't even sure how she knew she was done except, like a puzzle, things fit together. She could tell it was another person, on top of something. But the room wasn't as large as the garden, so she dragged a chair to stand up on it and get a better view of her puzzle-drawing.

When Evil stood on top of the chair, she recognized her great-great-great-grandfather immediately from family heirlooms they'd inherited. He wore black and he rode a horse. Cotton Mather was the man the witch, *maybe* Sarah Goode, was pointing at. The witch in her dream had thought this man had started it all. Evil felt sure this was a close-up of him looking at the pointing woman.

But what slowed Evil's heart was Cotton's face.

All of the pictures she had seen portrayed him as serene or wise or maybe even fatherly. This man on the horse looked very, very different.

The mouth had a hint of a smile, and the eyes...the eyes had this look of...excitement?

No.

Triumph.

Evil recalled how she felt as the woman in her dreams.

Weak. Dirty. Hungry. Pain.

Pain.

Pain.

A witch could be hungry? A witch could feel pain? Evil had never considered this. In her father's teachings, witches were bad and that was all.

Cotton Mather watched someone in pain, someone hungry, with an expression that was...

Then it fell from Evil's lips. A word she'd had to look up only once because it sounded like what it described to her.

"Smug." *He looks smug.*

She'd seen that look on the faces of all her school bullies.

The room grew dim and airless again, and she crouched on the chair, clinging to it, her head throbbing from both sleeplessness and understanding. With every thud of her growing headache, Evil heard her own realization:

The truth. The truth.

Ms. Goode is telling the truth.

CHAPTER 15—EVIL

The bonging of the clock tower awoke Evil. She abruptly sat up, blinking drowsily. People milled around nearby, unbothered by her sleeping self beneath the Narnia lamppost, surrounded by soft folds of white plastic and heavy, painted packages permanently scattered by the fawn's encounter with Lucy and fixed to the forever shiny bed of fake snow.

Davey.

She'd been waiting here for Davey, but...it was dark now. The lamppost glowed above her head, softened by the mist floating around it.

He should have been here hours ago.

She touched the straps of her backpack and tested its heaviness to make sure her drawings, as well as her sketchbook, were still with her. Then she drew her knees to her chest, shivering against the fog's dewy fingers.

He couldn't have gotten lost because he said he knew the spot.

Evil's heart curled. She hadn't even questioned whether he would show. All she'd thought about was everything she had to tell him. He would help her figure it out, come up with a plan or a next step.

At some point, she had not only decided to trust Davey, but she also depended on him.

Evil had spent most of her life being isolated and alone, focusing all her hopes on ending the Curse, being normal. She'd never pinned her hopes on another human being beyond her father.

And then that friendship she'd come to depend on without knowing it suddenly wasn't there. She hadn't known that missing someone was far worse than being alone.

The longer she sat there with *"he's not here, why isn't he here?"* playing on an endless loop in her head, the worse she felt.

She leapt up, determined to do something. If sitting there made her feel worse, then doing something might make her feel better.

What if Davey left me a note? Maybe he forgot something important at school and had to turn around and go back, and then it was too late to come here.

Evil ran up the stone steps and fled through the Time Tunnel until she burst upon the main desk area. Several people looked away as she approached. Barton hunched over his stack of binders and turned his back to her.

"Barton," she said in a normal voice, which sounded like shouting compared to everyone else. Heads turned, and a blushing Barton turned around, barely hiding his scowl. She pushed herself up on the counter, leaning forward so her feet dangled in the air behind her. "Has anyone left a note for me?"

"What? Like who?"

"Like...a boy? My age?"

The look on Barton's face said she had no chance of ever getting a note from a boy.

"No," he said simply and turned around to open a large binder.

"Is Ms. Goode here?" Evil asked, inspired.

"I haven't seen her," Barton replied without turning, squinting at something in the binder.

Evil's feet touched the floor. "Okay. Thanks," she mumbled. She wandered, dejected, staring at her feet.

She gasped as she bumped into a large cardboard sign, which tumbled to the floor. Several people looked her way as she stepped back from the rickety wooden stand that had propped up the sign. Evil picked it up and righted it again.

The sign, printed in heavy block letters, announced: THE UNVEILING OF COTTON MATHER'S LOST DIARY ON OCTOBER 31st. This was the event Ms. Goode meant, the one in which she would use a fake diary, a wooden one that would look like leather.

Two days from now. The day after the Anniversary, her special day, her "new beginning." The diary everybody wanted was right here, but nobody could read it.

Only a Mather can read the diary...

Her father had always told her that she wouldn't understand it, that he had studied Mather's works for years, that only he could read it.

But what if he was lying about that, too?

And what if there was no cure? What then?

What if...

But she didn't need to wonder. Ms. Goode didn't have to read the diary. Evil was a Mather. She could read the diary.

Her heart sped up. What Ms. Goode had told her suddenly rang true, and not just about the Mathers.

Evil had to get to the diary before her father to see if there really was a cure.

CHAPTER 16—DAVEY

102 days since the accident

Davey wore a groove on the playground as he paced during recess, thinking about Ava and her drawings. And while he had become used to not hearing much of anything at school except his name and "homework," now his ears also perked up when someone said "Johnny."

"I heard he had cancer," said a boy kicking a ball against a wall.

"I heard he won't wake up," said his friend.

Davey's shoulders sagged. He dreaded telling Ava, and he was surprised that he felt sorry for Johnny. He was a bully, but no one deserved this, did they?

Davey still pondered how to tell Ava about Johnny as he made his way to the Library after school. Just as he was about to turn off the sidewalk toward the green lawn of the Library, a heavy hand fell on his shoulder.

"You're Davey, aren't you?"

Davey stifled a gasp. He knew that voice.

The Reverend Mather blocked out the sun in his black robes. Davey stared up at the silver Mather crest around his neck, too scared to speak. The Reverend held Davey's gaze.

"Going to meet Evil?"

Davey shuddered when he said that word, that name. If he told the truth, would he get Ava in trouble? If he lied, would Reverend Mather know and force him to tell the truth?

"I'm afraid Evil is too tired to meet," the Reverend continued. "She's still asleep. But I do have an important message for you. Follow me."

The Reverend whipped around on his heel and walked at a swift pace. The billowing dark robe reminded Davey of a cape, but not the kind a hero wore. He ran after him. He couldn't risk missing an important message from Ava.

He had to trot to keep up with the Reverend's pace as he followed him around to the back entrance where Ava had retreated to the dryers. Reverend Mather charged up the stairs.

"Um, where we going?" Davey asked, panting, racing to keep up.

"Someplace we can talk privately." Reverend Mather's voice echoed in the stairwell.

Davey opened his mouth to ask why they couldn't talk right here, but the Reverend grabbed his hand and pulled Davey up the stairs. Davey stumbled. "Hey!" he protested, but the Reverend barely slowed until they reached the ninth floor.

They stopped before double doors that arched to a point in the middle, dark wood covered by vertical strips of black metal pierced by thick, knobby bolts. A small bronze sign read: *For ages 13 and Up.*

"I can't get in there," Davey said, relieved.

"You can if you're accompanied by an adult." The Reverend opened the door.

To Davey's surprise, it was darker than in the stairwell. He blinked as his eyes adjusted, but the Reverend pulled him firmly ahead. Long benches dotted with electric candles stood among the bookshelves. People with flashlights bent over the books, many with lace-up boots and long hair hiding their faces.

Reverend Mather abruptly dropped Davey's hand as they reached another room. He opened a door, and Davey reluctantly walked inside to a small, shadowy place where a tiny light only lit up the bookshelves. The door closed behind him.

Floor-to-ceiling bookshelves were lined with leather, gold-rimmed books with titles like *The Lair of the White Worm, We Have Always Lived in the Castle, The Thing on the Doorstep,* and finally, one that

Davey recognized, *Dracula*. The walls resembled enormous stones like the ones on the outside of the Library. A huge, red velvet chair sat beneath a fancy wall mirror in the corner nearest the door, opposite a tall painting of a smiling, elderly man with a pointed beard, wearing a black suit.

Davey swallowed hard. They were in the Horror section.

"One of my guilty pleasures, ever since Evil was born," the Reverend said, gesturing to the bookshelves. "I think I was drawn to this literature in an attempt to understand her." He nodded to the corner opposite Davey. "That's my favorite touch."

The Reverend pressed something on a nearby bookshelf, and a small light appeared, illuminating a full-sized coffin leaning against the wall.

Davey backed up against the velvet chair as he gawked at the coffin.

Reverend Mather stepped right up to it and opened it with a loud creak. Davey held his breath, but inside was only lined in white silk with red velvet trimming that matched the chair. But then, something else caught his eye: The silk looked different in places, a little darker at the top and in the middle, sunken and faded, like...like...

Like a body had been there.

Davey pressed himself against the bookcase, his fingers digging into the arm of the chair.

Reverend Mather grinned at him.

"I like this empty coffin so much better than if it had some vampire mannequin inside. This leads me to believe that the vampire is actually loose, roaming the Library, waiting in the dark for an unsuspecting victim."

Davey swallowed. "You said you had an important message from her," he mumbled, avoiding Reverend Mather's face.

He walked toward Davey, his grin evaporating. "I didn't say it was from her."

Davey's eyes darted toward the door. He was closer to it than Reverend Mather.

"You might be closer to the door than I am, Davey, but I am faster than you could imagine. You'll stay here until you've heard *my* important message."

Clearly her father had Ava's mind reading abilities. Davey resisted the urge to wedge himself behind the chair. The Reverend started to slowly pace.

"I've spent my life trying to help her. Do you know about her condition?"

Davey didn't say anything.

"She's a very sick little girl, with a long history of destruction. Evil believes her drawings are the cause of the destruction."

Davey's heart thudded in his ears.

"She's insisted on being called Evil from the time she could talk."

"Huh?" Davey squeaked.

The Reverend stopped and looked directly at Davey. "She would...hurt herself if I called her anything else. I didn't want her to come to harm. I finally gave in. I have called her Evil, as she wished, ever since."

He covered his face with his hands before continuing. "Can you imagine having to explain her condition to school staff? To get them to agree to call her that, knowing how other children would treat her?" He shook his head sadly.

Davey remained stock-still, wishing he could disappear. He looked up at the painting of the older man, but the eyes now glowed red, and he swiftly looked away.

The Reverend resumed pacing, the open coffin winking in and out behind his form as he passed in front of it. "Being unfit to teach her at home, I hired countless tutors to homeschool her. The tutors never stayed past the first day, and I was forced to release her to public schools. No medical doctors could find anything wrong with her, so I turned to psychology for help.

"I have spent years telling her the supposed Curse upon the Mathers during the Salem witch trials is responsible for her 'special' condition. Cotton Mather's lost diary was the key to it all, the key to lifting the Curse once and for all. It would reveal the full Curse and family secrets that would ensure she would never make anything bad happen again." He sighed. "And she would *want* a new name."

Davey blinked. *Curse?*

The Reverend rushed toward Davey and loomed over him. Davey cringed.

"I have spent my life convincing her that she has a chance to be normal. I have no other tricks up my sleeve. She only has to believe it to have a chance to be normal. But she does have to believe it." He stared hard at Davey. "Are you really going to deny her that?"

Davey gazed at the Reverend's knees, unable to meet his eyes. Ava *had* been so scared to be called something other than Evil. And she definitely believed her drawings made bad things come true.

But didn't Davey believe it as well?

The Reverend sighed again. He reached into his pocket. "I didn't want to have to do this, Davey, but I see you really need convincing."

Reverend Mather pulled something kind of big out of his pocket. Scared but curious, Davey craned his neck to see.

Davey sucked in his breath—a perfect miniature Davey lay in the Reverend's hands. From the curly hair and the brown skin to the way the figure had his hands stuffed in his pockets, it looked just like him.

"Evil made this recently," the Reverend said. "This is just one of many."

Davey recoiled. "But...she draws, she just draws!" he sputtered.

The Reverend nodded. "Yes, I thought that's all she did too." He looked at the figure. "She made these statues in her sleep, and I've let her think they are mine. I take this as a sign she's getting worse." His gaze darkened. "Do you have any idea *why* she might be getting worse?"

Davey swallowed but said nothing.

The Reverend regarded him through hooded eyes and slipped the statue back into his pocket.

"I know you are a broken child. So perhaps you were drawn to someone who is also broken. I can understand that." He paused. "But I want you to ask yourself, before you consider ever meeting her again: who are you really helping?"

And with that, the Reverend turned on his heel and left Davey in the room of Horror.

CHAPTER 17—DAVEY

102 days since the accident

Davey had only a fuzzy memory of leaving the Library, navigating his way through the thick rolling fog. Cars kept bursting out of misty clouds, startling him, but then he fell back into his thoughts.

His mother asked him right away what was wrong when he walked in the door of their apartment, a look of alarm on her face. Davey muttered about a stomachache and retreated to his room. To the space between the wall and the bed.

As he let the dark and quiet seep into his bones, soothing him, he argued with himself over what the Reverend Mather had said.

He's a liar.

Am I broken?

Is Ava broken?

He's a liar...isn't he?

But a small part of him whispered: *Did Ava make statues? Did she really make them in her sleep?*

Davey had always trusted the adults around him. It was hard to believe that a dad would lie this much. Because even when they had proof he hadn't been truthful about burning the drawings, Davey couldn't say why Ava's dad had fibbed.

But I still don't trust him.

Davey turned to the picture of his own dad on his nightstand.

"If you don't have anything else to hang on to, Davey, go with your gut. It's telling you something you've missed...or don't understand."

Davey closed his eyes and felt the bed give a little, just like when his dad would sit there. He sniffed, imagining him beside him. Davey could tell he'd had an easy shift because he only smelled like the office—coffee and stale muffins.

"Any theories?" his dad asked.

Davey shook his head. "I don't trust him, but I don't know why a dad would say these things. I don't get it."

Davey opened his eyes, and his dad vanished. As it sometimes did, the loss hollowed him out, made him a husk that could float away at any moment. Sometimes he wished he could.

"Why did you have to die?" he asked the picture on his nightstand.

The quiet and darkness that gave him peace in that space abruptly grew uncomfortable. Like he struggled to breathe. Davey pushed himself up and grabbed his backpack from the closet.

His ma looked up as she was setting the table. Guilt plucked at his insides. Davey used to set the table.

"Ma, I need some fresh air. I'm going for a walk, okay?" He grabbed a jacket from the hall closet.

"You're not hungry?" Her forehead creased. She reached into the basket of biscuits she'd put on the table and brought several to him. She put them in his hands and then bent down and hugged him. As bad as he felt, her hugs always made him melt a little, in a good way.

"You want to talk? Maybe we could drive somewhere?"

He cast his eyes down and shook his head.

"Then you stick to well-lit places and only places you know."

He smiled. It was a bit of a joke because Virtue was small enough that everyone knew pretty much every place. He put the food in his backpack.

"Okay, Ma. Thanks for the biscuits."

Out on the dark street dotted with tall lampposts that floated in the layers of fog, he wasn't sure where he was going except that he had a strong urge to leave. But no, not just leave. Go *somewhere*. Something tugged at him. He looked left and right on the big street that ran behind his apartment building. Toward school? Nope, the sensation said. The other way. So he turned toward downtown.

He passed the twenty-four-hour café, the 7-Eleven, and then as he neared Main Street, the *clop-clop* of horse hooves and a general buzz from all the tourists rose to his ears. As he turned left, couples in open horse-drawn carriages laughed and snuggled. Families paused before tiny restaurants, pondering the menus. A few people lingered in front of the bed and breakfasts, consulting their brochures or guides. A hint of chimney smoke wafted in the air, and Davey's stomach rumbled as he passed people in restaurants spooning pasta or slivers of meat into their mouths. As the shops, restaurants, and inns thinned, so did the people. Then there were no people.

The tugging feeling stopped abruptly like a rubber band gone slack.

Davey stood in front of the Virtue Police Station.

Like most places in Virtue, it used to be a house. A couple of stories, plus a basement, all red brick, with two big windows out front. They kept the blinds shut over most of the windows, except when Robby was on duty. He always kept the one nearest the receiving area open. He always said he liked to staff that area to "keep an eye on things," but Davey's dad had confided that he thought it was because Robby got lonely on his shifts at the front desk. Robby liked to talk, and often his coworkers found him talking to himself.

Robby had been his dad's partner.

Robby now stood at the tall desk in the entrance, writing something on a pile of papers, and his lips were pursed like he was whistling.

Davey moved out of Robby's line of sight, behind some tall hedges. He swallowed and his stomach growled. He took out the biscuits and finished them both in four massive bites, "chewing like a horse," as his ma said when he ate like that. When he'd swallowed the final bite, he took a deep breath.

Davey forced himself up the concrete path, but when he opened the door and heard the clack of the rolled-up blinds hitting the door at the top and smelled a warm, musty odor, he was surprised: It made him smile.

Davey hadn't known he missed this place. He stared from the dark green, white-flecked linoleum to the long, painful wooden benches, to the old-fashioned hanging lights, and finally to the shocked face of Robby and his wide-open mouth. Tears pricked at Davey's eyes, and he blinked them away.

It felt like he'd come home.

Robby found his voice. "Da—" It came out hoarse, and he cleared his throat. "Davey!" He shook his head, blinking in astonishment. "I just...I haven't seen you, uh..."

"Since the accident," Davey finished for him, and Robby's face relaxed a little.

Robby nodded. "Yeah." He paused, his eyes downcast, then looked up at Davey with his old goofy grin. He lifted the wooden divider of the front desk station and came out, thrusting his right hand toward Davey.

"Sir!"

Davey's hand collided with Robby's with a powerful *THOK!* Robby's eyes flared, and Davey wondered if he'd really hurt him this time, but he pumped Davey's hand as vigorously as always. Robby said "real men" had the hardest handshakes, so he challenged Davey to give him the hardest handshake he could every time they met.

"Sir!" Davey returned, with one final pump before dropping Robby's hand.

"Nice!" Robby commented, flexing his hand. He folded his arms and eyed Davey. "I think you're taller." He frowned like he was looking Davey over. "Yep, shoulders getting broader too. Soon you'll tower over me."

Davey gave a small smile, still having to crane his neck to look Robby in the eye.

"So what's the deal, Davey? You miss the smell of stale coffee and day-old baked goods?"

Yes. But that's not why he was there. Why was he here?

"I want to know why my dad...died." Heat flooded his face. It was true. That's why he was here.

Robby's eyebrows shot up. "Oh man, buddy." He rubbed the back of his neck. "I hate to disappoint you, but I don't know anything more than you read in the paper. The detective said it was cut and dry and closed the case pretty fast. Accidental homicide. The old guy was off his rocker because he hadn't taken his meds." He lifted his hands in a helpless gesture and dropped them again.

"I know"—Davey groped, not even sure what he was going to say next—"but why? Why did he stop taking his medication? Why did he shut himself up in his house and not go to work?"

Robby's mouth twisted in a funny way, but he gestured behind Davey to the two long ugly benches that had been harvested from an ancient school that was torn down. They framed a matching scarred coffee table in the middle that always had a mess of newspapers on it. Robby took the right bench, Davey the left. Like they used to.

Robby leaned forward, his elbows on his knees. "Doctor H was a weird old bastard—oh, sorry, Davey, my language." But he winked at Davey as he said this. "I think he had more books than friends. In fact, I think the books might have been his only friends. His own relatives barely knew him, didn't seem that concerned that he'd kicked off, I mean," he added hastily, "when they heard of his *demise*."

Despite the seriousness of the subject, the corners of Davey's mouth twitched. He always found it funny that Robby tried to speak in a proper way around him—but he liked that Robby didn't try too hard.

"Okay, so you're saying he was weird," Davey summarized. "But why did he go crazy *then*?"

Robby held up his hands. "Not a shrink." This was a trademark Robby response when he didn't understand something.

Davey stared at his hands, forcing himself to make connections he didn't want to. "I've...heard people talk about the diary."

"Speculation, but yeah," Robby said. "I thought you'd read it in all the papers."

Davey shook his head. "I didn't want to read anything about it." He hesitated. "So, what does it have to do with...that night?"

"It was in his house; clearly he'd been reading it and hadn't even told the Library they'd received it. Stuff like that."

"I wish I could read it," Davey said, to his surprise. "Yeah," he continued, looking at Robby intently, "I wish I could read it. Then maybe I would understand why he got so...crazy."

Robby turned his palms up and shrugged. "I don't know, Davey. It wasn't considered part of the crime scene since it was downstairs. The so-called expert the detective hired to look at Doctor H's notes got so sick he left before he could get anything meaningful out of them. All he said was that they looked like updated transcriptions from some of Mather's diary entries. And then the forensics came back, and it was open and shut."

Davey sat up straight. "Notes? Transcriptions?"

Robby's brow furrowed. "Doctor H wrote out some Mather diary entries in his own journal in modern English or something, which was on him when he was found. Now that the case is shut, we technically need to get them back to the Library." He rolled his eyes. "Oh, wait, that's on me. I need to call the Library, see if they want to come for them or if I should just, I dunno, make paper airplanes out of them." He smirked at Davey, but then his face fell.

"I'm sorry, Davey. I keep trying to lighten the mood, and by the look on your face, I've made you feel worse."

Davey snapped his jaw shut, hadn't even realized it was open until now. He shook his head. "You haven't made me feel worse. I just...I didn't know there were any notes. I mean...maybe they would tell me why this guy...why he did it." He licked his lips nervously. "Can I, uh, read his journal before you send them back to the Library?"

"Buddy, that's not up to me. They're Library property."

"Do you think the Library would let me read them then?"

"I'm not sure," Robby said. "You know, if you read them, they might make you feel worse. You never know."

"Nothing could make me feel worse."

Robby slapped his knee. "Okay then. The least I can do is get on the horn in the morning to the Library."

"How come you can't call 'em now?" Davey's heart beat faster. "Right now, while I'm here?"

Robby gestured to the window. "It's dark, they've probably—oh my God, I forgot they're a twenty-four-hour library, didn't I?"

He slapped his forehead as Davey nodded and grinned.

"Maybe I should read more," he said, standing up. "I'm on it. You stay right there, and I'll get you some rock-hard muffins in a moment."

He walked back to the front desk and picked up one of the black rotary phones while consulting a local phone book. Davey listened to the pleasant *swish-whirr* as Robby dialed each number.

"Yeah, this is Officer Rob Grendale at the station," he began, then paused. "The POLICE station, son. Okay, now, I am calling because I have some material connected to that old Mather diary. How would you prefer to get this stuff?" He listened and then snatched a nearby pen. "What's her number? You sure it's okay to call her at home? I'm going to tell her you said it's okay then. Thanks." He hung up, then held up a piece of paper.

"See? Things are already on their way. I'm going to call a Ms. Goode in the morning about these notes."

Ms. Goode...was this the same Ms. Goode that Ava had been talking about?

"You can't call her now?" Davey asked.

"Son, that Library might be open twenty-four hours, but I think it's safe to assume that Ms. Goode is closed for business right now." He frowned. "Wait. That came out wrong."

Davey didn't know what Robby meant, but he didn't care. All he could think about was finding Ms. Goode. She had to let him read the notes in that journal. She just had to.

And then it hit him: Somehow, he and Ava were both connected to this old diary. No matter what Reverend Mather said, Davey was heading back to The Library of Strange and Unusual Things tomorrow.

CHAPTER 18—EVIL

The Anniversary

Today's the Anniversary. *The most important day of my life. And I don't even know where he is.*

The Anniversary brought pain followed by hunger, luring Evil to their living quarters in the early hours of the morning. To her relief and confusion, perfect silence greeted her, but then she found a note pinned to her pillow. Evil's hand shook as she read it, her father's perfectly formed letters so straight and neat they could have been stenciled.

It is time at last, my dearest daughter. Meet me at 6:00 p.m. for your final trial.

Evil crushed the note and threw it into her backpack, still shaking.

Trial? What did he mean? And where was it? Did he have the diary? But most of all, her chest hurt because he didn't mention a cure. She still clung to a thin thread of hope and hated herself for it. *He did say "final" trial...*

But 6 p.m. was far away. She wasn't sure when she last slept more than a few hours. She couldn't even say when she last saw her father. She squeezed her eyes shut, forcing herself to focus on the two most immediate things after finding food:

1. Find Ms. Goode. She would know if her father had the diary.
2. Check the lamppost for Davey.

Once she had stuffed herself full of cereal, Evil questioned the Library staff, who said that Ms. Goode should be in already, but they hadn't seen her yet. So Evil started patrolling the main floor for an hour and then switched to sitting under the lamppost for an hour.

Whenever panic overtook her, her father appeared in her mind, frowning, shaking his head. *"I warned you, Evil. I warned you to respect the Curse. You always obeyed me before, but now, when it's most crucial..."*

Did he have the diary?

Once, Evil caught herself saying, "No! No! NO!" out loud, her hands over her ears. Fortunately, this was when she was beside the lamppost and not inside. But several parents shooed their children away from her.

The lack of sleep caught up with her. She knew it was lunchtime when she settled down with a granola bar on one of the larger packages around the lamppost—built so solidly that children could sit on them, she'd discovered—thinking she would just rest here for a moment.

She woke up, her head on her arms, half the granola bar on the ground between her legs. She grabbed it and lifted her head. The shadows of the lamppost and gifts all slanted sharply behind her, wavy on the folds of slick plastic snow. The clock tower bonged three times.

Three o'clock...Ms. Goode might have come and gone for all she knew! She shoved the half-eaten granola bar in her backpack and stood up but then caught her breath.

Davey sat cross-legged several feet away, next to the stairs. He stood up, too, and adjusted his backpack as he walked toward her, shoving his hands in his pockets. He had a guarded expression and kept looking away from her.

"I...I didn't want to wake you."

Evil stared, her throat tight. She forced her voice to be steady.

"Where've you been?" she asked softly.

"It's complicated," he said and then added, "I just mean...I'm not sure how to explain. But it was wrong of me to stand you up like that." He stuck out his hand to her and looked her in the eye. "I didn't mean to. I'm sorry, Ava."

Evil blinked, her eyes dry and achy, her nerves jittery. Shaking, she threw her arms around Davey. He grunted as she squeezed him.

"Thank you," she whispered into his ear, "for coming back."

She pulled back from him. "Davey, we have to find Ms. Goode."

"To tell her that you lied to your dad about her?"

"No." Evil shook her head and made a face. "So much has happened." She gave a weak smile as a tear dropped down her cheek. "I'm worried my dad might already have the diary and...he might lie. I might never know what's really in it."

Davey grabbed her hand. "But Ava, we might have the next best thing. Ms. Goode's getting a journal with the notes from the diary. I don't know if it will have what you want, but...it will...help me understand something really important."

"What?" Evil said, shaking her head. What had Davey just said? "Someone took notes on the diary?"

"I just found out last night." He looked down at his feet and withdrew his hand, shoving it in his pocket again. "I'm not interested in the...uh, way you're interested, but it's connected to something that happened to me. Something bad."

Evil lowered her voice. "The bad thing I felt when we met?"

Davey's eyebrows shot up, and then he nodded without looking at her.

"How?" Evil began, but Davey shook his head, lips pressed firmly together.

"I don't...I just...I don't want to talk about it, Ava, not yet."

He lifted his head, and her eyes met his. She nodded.

"Then let's both find Ms. Goode."

Evil and Davey asked at the front desk, but Barton said Ms. Goode was not to be disturbed.

"She's here!" both Evil and Davey said together and then exchanged embarrassed glances.

Barton glanced from Davey to Evil. "Yeah, and as I said, she can't be disturbed. She has an important and private affair to attend to."

Evil perked up and grinned. "Thank you, Barton." She tugged at Davey's sleeve to pull him to the hallways.

"Where're we going?" Davey asked as he followed her.

"To Ms. Goode," Evil answered quietly, leading him to a particular stairwell.

When they stood before the Community Room, all at once she heard her father's laughter. Deep like a growl—and rare. She swung around, but no one was behind her. Davey cocked his head at her. A cold fear coursed through Evil, and she rushed forward, bursting into the dimly lit room with Davey on her heels whispering "Ava!"

Ms. Goode shot up from the table, knocking over the bench and whipping around, her face wild.

She gasped, looking from Evil to Davey, who both stood rigid, their mouths open, staring back at Ms. Goode.

"What—" Ms. Goode began, putting her hand on her chest. "The door...the door was locked..." Her eyes darted between them.

Evil ran up to the librarian. "Ms. Goode! Julia! Are you okay? Are you okay?" Evil clenched her fists to her chest in anxiety.

"Other than losing a year of my life to that entrance?" Ms. Goode asked, taking a final deep breath. She bent down and righted the bench.

Evil whimpered, and Ms. Goode took her gently by the shoulders. "I didn't mean it, I promise. Why do you think I would not be okay?"

"I...I just felt like something horrible was going to happen," Evil sputtered, not wanting to explain the laughter she alone heard. "Ms. Goode, does my father have the diary?"

"No, it's still being restored. I'm actually very surprised that he hasn't even asked for it." Ms. Goode stood aside and pointed at a journal lying on the table. "But as it so happens, these are the notes from the diary. Modern transcriptions, I was told, of several diary entries."

*He hasn't even asked for it. But...that's why we moved here. That's what this entire day is for...*Evil fell silent, unable to understand what she was hearing.

"That's it? The notes are in there, for real?" Davey cut in and moved toward the table where the journal sat, but Ms. Goode put up a protective hand. He looked up at her, puzzled.

"You are surely Davey," Ms. Goode said, extending her hand. A surprised Davey shook it.

"Sorry, uh, Ms. Goode," Davey apologized. "I should have introduced myself."

"Ava and I have talked quite a bit recently," she explained. "That's how I guessed."

Davey looked at Evil. "Did you tell her to call you Ava?"

Evil gave a hesitant smile. "It's complicated. She knows a lot."

"Rob told me you might be asking about the journal," Ms. Goode said to Davey. She looked at Evil. "Davey is why we have these notes at all."

"You are?" Her jaw dropped, momentarily distracted from her grim thoughts.

"You're catching flies," Davey said with a small grin. "I can explain later too. Um, Ms. Goode?"

"Julia is fine, Davey," she said with a smile and gestured at both Davey and Evil to sit at the bench on either side of her.

"Thanks...uh, Ms. Goode." He cleared his throat. "So, have you read them already?" He glanced around. "Though it'd be pretty hard to read in here with it so dark and all."

"No, I haven't read them." The librarian looked at Evil. "I was going to find Ava first, but it looks like I don't have to now."

"Ms. Goode," Evil said, realizing she still wanted to know what the diary said, no matter what, "I...I want to read Dr. Hathorne's journal. I know you don't believe anything bad can happen, but, well, there are lots of reasons I think I should read them." She gazed meaningfully at the librarian, hoping she remembered about the cure.

Ms. Goode opened her mouth, then closed it again. She nodded slowly. "You're right, Ava. And of course no one believes anything would happen to you, as a Mather."

"Huh?" Davey glanced from Evil to Ms. Goode.

"Only a Mather can read the diary," Evil reminded him.

"I don't get it. Plus, these are notes or transcriptions or whatever," Davey protested.

Ms. Goode continued. "I don't believe the diary can harm anyone, but it is true that my mother lost her life in search of this diary."

Davey inhaled and took a step back in shock. "Oh," he stammered. "Oh."

"Yes, my interest is personal," Ms. Goode explained. "There is a belief that only a Mather can read the diary, that something bad will happen to a non-Mather who attempts to read it." She sighed. "I find that a very convenient thing for Mathers to promote. Many who descended from those accused of witchcraft at Salem have lost their lives to the Mathers without any contact with the diary at all."

Davey glanced at Evil. "They did?"

"Of course," the librarian continued, "the fact that Dr. Hathorne died reading the diary has stoked a belief in its power all over again."

"Dr. Hathorne?" Evil asked Ms. Goode, then glanced at Davey with a puzzled expression.

Davey's face grew pained, and he ducked his head.

Ms. Goode's eyes darted from Davey to Evil. "The last person to read the diary. And he didn't survive."

"Oh," Evil said in a small voice.

"Despite the fact that I do not believe only a Mather can read the diary or, in this case, notes therein"—she paused, glancing at Evil—"this right really belongs to Ava much more so than me, especially on the Anniversary."

Evil's throat swelled and her eyes burned.

"Anniversary of what?" Davey asked.

"Father said it's when the witch cursed—" Evil broke off, casting an apologetic glance at Ms. Goode, who mouthed "*it's okay*" in return. "This lady accused of witchcraft cursed my great-great-great-grandfather, Cotton, in July, and he had a divine inspiration on how to defeat it in October. The Mathers call the day Cotton had the inspiration the Anniversary," Evil explained.

"Oh. Uh, do you know what was in the curse?" he asked cautiously.

"We think it's in the diary. Tonight was..." Evil's voice trailed away, and she covered her face. "I was supposed to be cured of the lady's Curse today. After Father read the diary. He thinks it has the cure." *But he hasn't even asked for the diary...*

Davey cleared his throat and pushed his hands into his pockets.

"You think you're cursed?" Davey asked, not looking Evil in the eye.

"Father always told me I was," she said. She wanted to mention her drawings and Johnny, but she feared what Ms. Goode would think.

"When does the Anniversary take place? So much of the day is already over," Ms. Goode observed.

"At six o'clock." The more she spoke about the Anniversary, the worse she felt.

"What happens at six?" Davey asked.

"I don't know," Evil said in a small voice.

"I thought the diary had to be involved?" Ms. Goode asked.

"Me too," Evil said, raising her sad eyes to Ms. Goode's. "But I want to know if he was telling the truth at all about the cure."

"Do you know where your father is, Ava?" Ms. Goode asked, her tone concerned.

Evil shook her head. "Not...yet."

The librarian stood up. "If you both can stay for an hour or two, I think Ava could read these notes out loud to us. And then, then I think we'll all know what to do." But Ms. Goode didn't sound completely convinced to Evil. The librarian strode to one wall and pressed a button, allowing golden light to settle lightly in the center of the room, just enough to see by.

Davey squinted toward the far end of the room. "Is that...a bale of hay?" He pivoted his head left and right. "And it looks like someone wrote all over the walls."

"All in good time, Davey," Ms. Goode said, pulling out the bench and patting his hand. "Ava?" Ms. Goode gestured to the journal and folded her hands together, lowering her head like she was going to pray.

Evil locked eyes with Davey before she nodded and reached out a shaking hand to open the journal.

She turned the first page, making a faint rustling sound as she did. Her attention fell on the Library motto at the top of the page, *Evolutionis Doctrina*. Evil briefly closed her eyes and made a wish.

Let me be cured! Let me learn, let me evolve!

Evil opened her eyes and concentrated on the page. Then blinked. She squinted.

"Excuse me," she said, pushing out the bench and going right under the light. She held the journal right up to her nose, then far away.

"Are you alright, Ava?" Ms. Goode asked.

Evil pressed the journal to her chest, tears springing to her eyes. "M-Ms. Goode. I can't...I can't read it!" The last word came out like a hoarse cry.

Ms. Goode frowned, then understanding spread over her face as her head righted itself. She sighed. "He wrote in cursive, didn't he?"

"Uh-huh," Evil said, still clutching the journal.

"The entire staff was required to either type or write in block script. Dr. Hathorne fought this tooth and nail, and so there were many years that I had to interpret his handwriting, his unique cursive." She rubbed her eyes again, then dropped her hands. "I will have to read the journal."

"NO!" Evil cried. "You CAN'T!"

Ms. Goode stood up and went to her, bending down on one knee and putting her hands over Evil's.

"Ava, listen to me. I don't believe in superstition. I was happy to let you read the journal because I know it's important to you, but I'm not afraid to read it. Do you believe me?"

Evil gazed into Ms. Goode's pleading eyes. She knew Ms. Goode believed what she was saying...but did she?

"I'll try," Evil whispered.

"I can't ask for more than that," the librarian said, standing.

Ms. Goode reached out and slowly withdrew the journal from Evil's hands. She went to the buffet and returned with matches, lighting the fat candle that rested in the center of the table with a shaking hand. "No real candles are allowed anywhere else in the Library, but lighting one with others present is a Community ritual."

She took her place at the center of the table. Evil scrambled behind her and put her hand on her shoulder. The librarian smiled and patted Evil's hand with hers.

"I can stand behind you and try to follow along," Evil said. "Maybe it will help."

Ms. Goode lowered her eyes. "Thank you, Ava."

The librarian exhaled, her fingers landing lightly on the journal. With her other hand, she reached into her bag and withdrew her inhaler. She held it to her lips and gave a quick puff.

Then her fingers closed down on the cover of the journal.

"Here we go, children," she whispered.

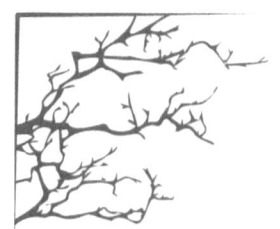

CHAPTER 19

Dr. Hathorne's Transcriptions: Select Entries of Cotton Mather's Diary

1691 [December] **Boston**

This year finds me, the Lord's humble servant, manufacturing miracles of God's will through my gift, my clay miniatures.

It was not until recently, however, that I discovered the ultimate purpose for my divine gift, a miraculous revelation.

After three days of fasting from all food and drink, I had a vision of claws in darkness, toothed mouths, and rolling, bloody eyes. But most of all the claws—snatching good people's spirits right out of them so they fell where they stood, nothing but shells without their souls.

I was terribly frightened until I realized that I was being shown my path, that it was my destiny to work against the greatest of evils: *Witchcraft*.

And lo, my path unfolds: Today, I received word from the Reverend Samuel Parris that I am needed at Salem Village. Reverend Parris must tend to his sick daughter, Elizabeth, and would be *most grateful* if I, a man of God for whom he held such great respect, would consider serving as a guest minister in his time of need. A villager had been suffering from possession, and his flock needed reassurance they had *God's protection* whilst he tended to his daughter, Elizabeth, with the aid of his niece, Abigail.

I am making many notes for my sermons as I am preparing to leave for Salem. But, before I leave, I regard it as prudent to sculpt a miniature of Parris based on a portrait. Witchcraft can grip even the saintliest of men, and *who knows what will happen* once I arrive.

1692, [January] Salem Village

I came to Salem just a few weeks hence, and it has been a most strange experience. Salem behaved like a typical village with its modest housing bordered by forest. Faithful, humble villagers able to quote scripture upon command. But that is where the ordinary stopped.

Firstly, my sermon notes disappeared within my second day. I was walking past the church with some difficulty as the snow had become icy mud, and I nearly walked right out of my shoes several times. Finally, I paused, exhausted. I reached into my pocket to fetch my handkerchief. Out of habit, I sought to touch my sermon notes, which I kept with me always, as I did the clay Parris miniature. The moment my hand closed upon air in my pocket where the notes should have been, my breath left me. Then a voice spoke at my back:

"Sir, have ye lost something? If I helps ye to find it, would ye share some bread with me?"

I turned, my hand still in my pocket, clutching air and not my sermon notes. Near me stood a woman, visibly with child, her belly round under her skirts. Long strands of dark brown hair dripped out of her dirty white cap, and her face, though comely, was also marred by grime. But what struck me were her hands. She had a hand held out to me, a shy smile playing on her face. But the hand, the fingers, the nails! It looked much like a claw to me.

She must have noticed my stare because she hastily wiped her hand on her skirts. "Sorry, sir, the blisters are from chopping wood. Me hand curls up like this for a while."

Distressed about my notes and this sudden appearance of this woman at the same time, I nonetheless tried to be like the Lord: forgiving. I pointed to the church.

"There is a small loaf of bread in there that I have yet to bless," I said. "It is behind the curtain, and you tell those in attendance that I said you may have it."

She whispered a prayer of thanks as she lurched, both due to the mud as much as her condition, toward the church. I crossed myself, hoping one with child would not be dealing in witchcraft and stealing my sermon notes. When I told this tale to Parris, he recognized her as Sarah Goode. Poor but harmless, he said. Yet I wondered...

I hadn't been there in Salem more than a week when it became clear that it was not just any neighbor who was possessed but *that of Samuel Parris's daughter, Elizabeth*. She was mute and frozen in her manner, and Parris sent her to recover with relatives. Yet she had hardly departed when Parris's niece, Abigail Williams, became afflicted in a much different manner. She screamed at the sight of the good book, and when asked to recite scripture, she babbled and rolled on the ground, gouging her eyes with her fists. I did not leave the Parris house for four days, holding vigil with Abigail, but still she raved. The Reverend Parris and I set out of his house to consult about this matter on a walk.

We had only taken a few steps beyond his house when Sarah Goode, the one with child, accosted us. She waved something over her head.

"Reverend Mather, Reverend Mather!" she cawed, flapping her spindly arms like crow wings from under her dirty—perhaps once white—shawl. She labored up to us, panting, one hand clutching something, the other holding the small of her back.

"Reverend Mather!" she repeated, thrusting something toward us. "I saws it drops from your pocket in the morn', but I couldn't reach it for some time with me belly, and by then, ye was too far away."

To my great horror, she held my miniature of Parris in her filthy claw. The reverend gasped and he looked from *me to her*. I stared at her claw, the blackish nails, the reddened knuckles, the stretched skin. I pleaded in my heart for the Lord to tell me how to keep His secret safe. *Please,* I begged, *protect your divine son!*

He answered me completely. And spoke through me.

She had given me the tool with which to reveal the truth I suspected.

I stepped in front of Parris and shielded him with my arms.

"Why have you made an image of your reverend? What are you trying to inflict upon him?"

Sarah's arm lowered, her face changed from happiness to surprise.

"But...it's not mine. Only a great talent could make such a thing!" And she held up my miniature again to me but more feebly this time.

I thrust one arm into my pocket, touched the miniature of Parris's niece that I had finished last night, and plunged my thoughts into her.

Behind us, the front door slammed open against the side of the house, and Abigail flew out before us. Her eyes wild, her bonnet askew, she pointed at Sarah.

"Stop hurting me! I cannot bear it and will not drink blood with you! Leave me be! Leave us all be, Sarah Goode!"

The filth...the claws...I knew it, as did the Lord, speaking through Abigail: Sarah Goode had been a witch all along.

Abigail fell and writhed on the ground, only the whites of her eyes showing, her back arching in a most unnatural way as froth poured from her mouth. The reverend dropped to the ground, grabbing his niece and shouting her name, though she seemed not to hear him.

I pulled myself up to my greatest height and said in my most ministerial tones:

"Sarah Goode, by the power of the Lord Almighty, I hereby accuse you of *witchcraft*!"

The reverend and I dragged Sarah Goode to the constable. He confined her in the jail after witnessing the miniature and hearing our tale. I insisted upon keeping the miniature for study, which the reverend and the constable were glad to oblige, both shuddering mightily upon seeing it.

All the way to the constable, Sarah had cried that she was no witch.

Of course, that is exactly the falsehood a witch would claim.

1692, [May] Salem Village

It has been a many trying month. The only bright spot has been the news from my wife that she discovered in February that she is expecting. God be praised. I cling to this good news. Because all my other doings are combatting darkness here in Salem.

While Sarah Goode remains in jail, Abigail claimed another local woman was torturing her with her spirit. I therefore realized that witchcraft was spreading. I knew there had to be more witches and had a divine epiphany.

Prophets. Through my gift, the Lord had led me to a young prophet in the form of Abigail, and she had revealed Sarah Goode to be a witch. But to rely on a solitary girl was unreasonable. It took several weeks to identify the girls I sensed were seers, dig up the clay, and make their miniatures. And through the miniatures, the Lord brought forth the ability to identify witches in these prophet girls.

I had since prudently made a miniature of Sarah Goode, telling her likeness that if she confessed and named other witches, she would likely be released to do penance and have her child. Yet to my horror, when I visited her, she resisted the Lord's will: She did not confess, not even when her husband and Dorcas, her daughter of only five years of age, testified against her.

Not even when Dorcas herself was put in jail for witchcraft.

1692, [June] Salem Village

The prophet girls identified so many witches, I fear the accused could use their power collectively to break free from jail, perhaps even leave Salem and infect another village nearby. Parris suggested marking them in some way as a warning to all, and I said yes, but in a way they cannot disguise nor remove.

For those found guilty, Parris and I blessed a farming instrument that became an instrument of God. I prayed loudly over their sinful screams as they branded the guilty witches. I prayed that they might release their pact with Satan so as to end their pain.

And I went to Sarah Goode for the last time. I carried my candle to where Sarah was confined—in a coffin cell, of course, with only enough room to stand and not even a bucket because she had no one to pay for it. I had to raise the candle high to observe a creature once human, crouched as much as she could with her knees against the door.

Those huge eyes emerged from blackness, the claws reached up to the bars, the iron ankle chain scraping the ground as she moved...I now was certain of my vision many months ago, when the Lord chose my path. Her eyes swallowed her sunken face, the cheeks withered, the lips parched and shriveled. Her entire body shook as she stood.

She held her weeks-old babe swaddled in rags in one of her quaking, spindly arms, but it was strangely quiet. Sarah's other arm clutched at the bars, the ragged nails bloody, the hand all knobs and points. Her claws tightened around the babe when she saw me, the brand on her right arm a bloody color that oozed yellow bile. I reached into my pocket and touched her miniature.

"You have something to tell me, child."

She spat through the bars, jostling her newborn babe, who whimpered.

"I have nothing to tell ye!" she rasped.

She turned her face away, and I stood back in disgust.

"What kind of mother lets her babe suffer!"

"What kind of man be falsely accusing mothers?" she countered so fast I nearly stumbled over a three-legged stool behind me. I grabbed it and pointed the stool at her in my anger, shaking it.

"You will confess or you will hang!" My words rang in the cell, and all at once the others fell silent.

She turned to face me and held the babe tight, thrusting her face into the bars. Her quivering, bloodshot eyes found mine.

"I will hang no matter *what* I say."

1692, [July], Salem

I have witnessed many hangings of witches, and yet Salem still suffers. Witches have died in jail, but Salem still suffers. But today, July 19, I suffered most of all.

The Lord smote Sarah Goode in every way He could: Her infant died, and her young daughter Dorcas remained jailed. Still, Sarah did not confess.

Today, Sarah hanged.

But she did not go quietly.

When they drew the cart up under the gnarled tree and pulled the noose around Sarah's neck, she wavered on the ladder. I stopped on my horse at a respectful distance and put my hand in my pocket to touch her miniature and held my breath. *You will confess. They all do.*

Even at a distance from her, she locked eyes with me. I question whether I could move had I wanted. With the rope around her neck, she stretched out her arm and pointed at me. The crowd went quiet, and all turned to me. Then, damn that witch, she spoke.

> *From this day forward*
> *Only sons will Mathers bear*
> *God-play comes at a heavy price*
> *Of this prophecy beware:*
> *Evil will fell you*
> *End the Mather line*
> *Dark promise of tomorrow*
> *Virtue will be the final sign*

The crowd gasped. Her miniature snapped in two in my pocketed hand, and the jailer jerked the ladder from under Sarah's feet. Sarah Goode's legs scrabbled in the wind, and her life began to end. The witch struggled to keep hold of her wicked life for what seemed like eternity itself. More than any other, she wheezed, she flailed, she clawed at her throat. Her legs kicked, and the most awful of sounds came from her. But her eyes would not leave me. And I would not leave that spot until her limbs, after much time, finally ceased moving.

1692, [October], Boston

As I write this, only three months since I returned from Salem, the evidence of Sarah Goode's Curse lies beside me: my dead infant daughter.

What had I done wrong to be cursed? How had I displeased the Lord? *Punish ME and not my baby girl*, I cried, and forced myself to walk up and down the stairs on my knees as penance until they were so bruised I could not hold my yells. I went to our basement, cold enough to make me blue, dark enough to shroud my vision. I slashed my palm with a knife. I clasped my hands together, squeezing hard to make it flow. Weeping, I lowered my head to the floor and held up my bloody hands to show contrition. I then lay prone for countless hours, offering myself to the Lord, to do with me what He will.

Let me make amends, I begged, *show me how I've failed you that you allow this Curse to grip me so!*

Shaking with chill and hunger, not knowing whether it was day or night, images formed before me in the darkness: Sarah Goode's daughter, Dorcas, being carried from the jail. She kicked and screamed in the arms of Goode's husband. He whispered, "You're free now, everything will be as it was, you're free..." but she thrashed and howled and tried to bite him. He slapped her hard, but instead of crying, she fell limp in his arms, her eyes vacant, her hair limp and greasy against her small skull.

This vision was replaced by a young man weeping under the hanging tree. By his black hair and torn breeches, I recognized him as the younger son of that *queen of hell* Martha Carrier that I'd heard hanged in August. I could still hear her rasping voice, see her snaggle tooth. Yet her son wept for this hag.

This image melted into a boy whose dark skin immediately marked him as the bastard of Martha and Giles Cory. Both witches, both dead, God curse their wicked souls. He sat with his head in his hands on the very spot where Giles had been pressed to death under many stones.

And then I was again in the basement, alone. I stood up, grateful for the pain throbbing in my knees, pulsing in my hand. I held up my hands and closed my eyes, weeping. The Lord had shown me how to gain his forgiveness and, most important, how to fight Sarah Goode's Curse.

These witches had spawned. They, the guilty witches, might have died, but their blood—*unlike mine*—lived on. Their sons and daughters were likely just as tainted. If I made their miniatures, the Lord would tell me so through them.

I could eliminate the Curse by eliminating this evil. I had left Salem far too soon! I needed to alert my Mather brethren of the threat to us and how we must combat it. We must use our gift collectively toward this righteous goal. Sarah Goode had, after all, cursed the line. None of us were safe. My family needed to know and needed to protect themselves.

I have been blinded by my grief to the larger workings of this Curse, but I am lifted from grief with the revelation on how to destroy it. Sarah Goode started a war against the Mathers. But the Mathers would end it. We would end her people—and her fellow witches. Virtue was the final sign? It would be *our sign* because there can be nothing more virtuous than our mission: the destruction of evil.

I mark this day, the 30th of October, a day to be celebrated among Mathers. A day when our true purpose arrived.

We would exterminate the lines of the witches, *however long it took*.

CHAPTER 20—EVIL

The Anniversary

Ms. Goode's voice hoarsely uttered the last word of the final page Dr. Hathorne had scrawled from Cotton's diary. She silently closed the journal, pressed her palms to the table, and lowered her head.

Evil and Davey sat mute, Davey's arms wrapped around himself, Evil's legs drawn up to her chest, only her hair and wide eyes showing above the collar of Davey's jacket.

Red wax wept down the sides of the shrunken candle, pooling around the base and edging over the sides onto the table.

Ms. Goode's wet eyes blinked slowly at Evil, and then she blew out the candle.

"Cotton was the...it was Cotton." The librarian's throat contracted and bobbed as she choked out the words. The librarian gazed with seriousness at Evil. "The...clay statues...your father...I think your father believes he has the same...gift. It would explain why he's been making them."

Evil thought of the statues in her father's workshop in the lower levels of the Library. Could he do what Cotton did? She remembered his crumpled, weeping face when she spied on him as a toddler. Crying over the statues of her. Something shifted in her like a bone snapping into place.

Was he...had he been trying to...control her? Through those statues? Way back then? And then he stopped, he stopped making the statues a long time ago...until we got here. Until we got here...

The librarian's mouth trembled. "I think...that's why...the Mathers interpreted the curse the way they did. They could never believe that

Cotton Mather, that he was the one. Because Cotton himself didn't believe it. He thought his will was...divine."

"I don't understand," Evil whispered, looking at Davey, who remained quiet, still staring at the dark candle.

A tear ran down Ms. Goode's cheek, then another, and another. "Cotton believed he was getting people to do what God wanted them to do. But all they were doing was what *Cotton* wanted them to do."

"But how?" Evil asked.

"I can't exactly say. But Cotton created the witch hunt. That's all. And that's everything." Ms. Goode leaned down and pulled a tissue out of her bag and dabbed her eyes.

"Not Sarah Goode," Davey whispered. "Cotton didn't get Sarah to do anything."

Ms. Goode and Evil looked at him, but he kept his head down.

"You're right, Davey," the librarian said.

"You think," Davey went on, "he could make people do stuff? Through his clay people?"

For a moment Ms. Goode was quiet, then she dug into her purse and held out what looked like a Barbie doll at first to Evil, but when the librarian laid it on the table, it made a clinking sound. Ms. Goode removed her hand, and both Davey and Evil cringed.

A statue of a woman with long black hair and big blue eyes wearing a blue pants suit lay on the table. Every line on her face, even the veins in her hands, was so detailed; it was like a real person had been shrunk down to size.

"This was my mother," Ms. Goode said quietly. "She traveled to Boston to meet someone who said they had information about Cotton's diary. She was the Director here," Ms. Goode explained. "She never came back. A week after her funeral, I got this figure in the mail without a return address, but it did have a note."

Ms. Goode removed a pocketbook from her purse. Opening the pocketbook, she ran a finger along an inside fold and pulled out a piece of paper. She read: *"Your mother died in a very long war that a few of us have tried to end. I think only the diary, which has all the answers, can end it, but this will provide a clue to the truth."* Ms. Goode sighed. "I didn't know what they meant until now. But I refuse to believe that statues alone can do anything."

"But Cotton said—" Davey protested.

"What we just heard," Ms. Goode interjected, "was what Cotton believed. I believe he had an incredibly strong will." Her eyes fell on her mother's clay likeness. "I don't believe they can do anything on their own."

Evil fought a sudden urge to lie down, to sleep instead of wrestle with these problems. Maybe if she woke up, she would be back in Boston, back when finding the diary was all about the cure for the Curse. Her throat bobbed as she tried to swallow her disappointment.

"There was nothing in the notes about a cure." Evil's voice came out in a croaky whisper.

After a brief silence, Ms. Goode agreed. "No, there's not, Ava. I know you must feel terribly disappointed, but..." The librarian paused. "I'm so sorry. I just wish you didn't believe you needed a cure. I wish you could see yourself like Davey and I see you."

"You really believe you're cursed," Davey muttered, and Evil turned to him in surprise.

Ms. Goode put her hand over Evil's. "Ava, you're looking at the curse through Mather eyes. We really don't know what it meant. Virtue can mean many things; so can the word *evil.*"

"But Sarah Goode said...about sons...and I'm the first girl in the Mather line since 1692." Evil bit her lip to keep from crying.

Ms. Goode hesitated. "Ava, how could it be evil to end a centuries-long genocide? That's what your birth did, whether we understand how or not. Something...impossibly good...happened for the Community when you were born. We started to live."

Davey stood up so fast he nearly fell over, and Evil and Ms. Goode jumped. He pointed his finger at the statue.

"So maybe this dumb thing doesn't mean anything now is what you're saying? It can't hurt me?"

Davey's coat had fallen to the floor. Evil slowly picked it up, eyeing Davey warily.

"Davey, why would a statue of my mother hurt you?" Ms. Goode frowned, puzzled.

"There's a statue that looks like me. I saw it." Davey slowly turned to Evil. "And he said *you* made it."

Evil sucked in her breath. "You've talked to Father?"

"He found me. It's why I didn't show up that day."

Evil's heart fluttered like a frantic bird. "Davey, I've never made them! Father did. But ...he'd stopped for a long time...until we got here." She cast a guilty look toward the librarian, who raised her eyebrows.

"Did you know he made a statue of me?" Davey asked, his fists clenched.

Evil gave a hesitant nod.

"And you didn't tell me." His eyes darkened.

Evil swallowed hard, looking from Ms. Goode to Davey. "I was afraid. I didn't know what it meant. Father said it had to do with my cure, the Anniversary—"

"What if I need a cure, Ava?" Davey interrupted. "You ever think of that? You ever think you're not the only one who wants to be cured of something?"

Evil stepped back, crushing his coat in her arms. Ms. Goode stepped toward Davey.

"Davey, I don't think she knows; she won't understand your anger."

"Know what?" Evil asked, glancing from Ms. Goode to Davey.

Davey's jaw jutted out, his hands still balled into fists at his sides. "She knows something bad happened to me, that much I know. She said it the first time we met."

"I felt it, Davey," Evil said in a soft voice, desperately searching his face. "I don't know how it happened, but I felt that you had lost someone. Why are you mad? What should I know?"

Davey pointed an accusing finger at the journal. "That's how it happened! The stupid diary! Dr. Hathorne was reading that diary and taking those notes, and he went crazy and shot my dad when he came to check on him. That's what happened, Ava."

A small whimper escaped from Evil's throat.

"All these notes prove is that my dad died for nothing. If you're so special, do something good for a change: Make my dad come back."

"Davey!" Ms. Goode gasped.

Davey ran past them and flung open the door with a bang.

And then he was gone.

Ms. Goode followed Evil back to her quarters. She clutched Davey's coat in her arms, as if she feared it might disappear too.

"Ava, we need to talk more. But it will be six o'clock soon—isn't your father expecting you? He shouldn't see you with me."

"Ms. Goode, I haven't seen my father for days."

"Days?" Ms. Goode asked, her face full of alarm. "Where is he?"

"I don't know, Ms. Goode. I don't know anything." She paused at the door to their passageway and looked up at Ms. Goode.

Ms. Goode put her hand on Evil's shoulder. "Ava, I can't imagine how devastating that was, hearing who Cotton really was, what he did."

Evil unlocked the door. "My father lied my whole life." Her voice sounded calm to her, almost like someone else was speaking. "My whole life is a lie." Evil stared into the dark hall. She should be upset. Why wasn't she upset? Instead, her limbs weighed her down, urging her to rest and sleep. And when she fought this urge, she watched everything from above: *There goes the librarian with the red-haired girl...*

It was like someone was playing the movie of her life, and her heart thudded with fear as she wondered what would happen next. What possibly could be more horrible around the corner?

Be careful, she silently shouted at the girl beside the librarian. *Watch out, he could be anywhere!*

He? Who's he? Her own inner voice sounded strange, hollow.

Ms. Goode kneeled in front of her, startling Evil out of watching her life movie, bringing her back inside it. Ms. Goode's voice slightly reverberated in the uncarpeted hall.

"Your father didn't lie, Ava. The entire Mather Clan embraced that perspective of the curse. A curse they couldn't even properly remember. It started with Cotton."

"So he didn't lie," she repeated dully, "but he chose to name me Evil because he believed I was going to destroy the Mathers." She gazed at the librarian. "Which is worse, Ms. Goode?"

The librarian squeezed Evil's shoulder and stood up. "One thing at a time. What is it you wanted to find here? May I help?" She walked into their dining room, looking around.

"I want to show you something." Evil opened the door to her room, flicking on the light and dropping her backpack, laying Davey's coat gently on her bed. Ms. Goode gasped and put her hand on her chest.

"Oh...oh." Her eyes darted around the room nervously. "Ava, what are...these drawings?"

"They're mine." Evil turned away from Ms. Goode to rifle through some drawings around the doorframe.

"These are all things...you dreamt about?" the librarian asked.

"No. My father asks me to draw a lot, but sometimes I also drew what I felt before he helped me to control it." Evil didn't need to close her eyes to imagine the slippery feel of the silk around her wrists.

"Your father asked you to draw some of these things?"

"He would tell me a story and then ask a question about the person in the story. My drawings would answer his question. I never knew what I was going to draw."

"But why? Why would he ask you something and expect you to draw an answer? To what end?"

"My drawings make things happen. Bad things." Evil turned around to face her. "But you don't believe in Sarah Goode's Curse, right?"

"I think the curse is whatever people believe it to be." Ms. Goode's eyes lingered on the drawings. "And," she continued, then stopped. Evil followed her gaze. Ms. Goode stared at the drawing of Lawrence's hands.

The librarian turned to Evil. "I remember seeing you when Lawrence had that reaction. What made you draw his hands?"

"I didn't mean to. Father told me a story about how Lawrence could get hurt if he read the diary and how much his wife needed him. He asked how we could keep him from getting hurt, and this is what I drew."

"Keep him from getting hurt? His hands..."

"But he's alive."

Ms. Goode startled, then exhaled sharply. "To answer your question, Ava: No, I don't believe in curses. I believe human beings are capable of quite enough good and..." She hesitated, looking at some of the drawings. "...horrible things. They don't need curses."

"But Cotton's gift?" Evil asked. "And you believe everything changed when I was born. It sounds like you believe in something."

"I only know what Cotton and the Mathers believed," Ms. Goode corrected, her eyes sad. "And I know what happened to my Community and how everything changed with your birth, even if I don't understand it. I only suspect your birth had a profound effect on the Mathers." She sighed. "I've seen what happens when people believe in evil. I choose to believe in goodness."

Evil sat with what Ms. Goode said, not certain she fully understood. "Do you think Cotton made things happen with those...miniature things?"

"I can't believe it, no. Clearly he believed it. His belief spurred the witch hunt."

"Does that mean you think my drawings don't do anything? Good or bad?"

Ms. Goode looked down, then back at Evil.

"Ava, you might as well ask me to believe in witchcraft. I won't believe you can make bad things happen with your drawings. I'm shocked to hear it. What I do know is that you are the only thing associated with the cessation of genocide in the Community. That's what matters to me."

"Ms. Goode, for as long as I can remember, my father has asked for my help through my drawings."

Ms. Goode's brow furrowed. "Help? That's how he said it? He asked you to draw...to help him?" She sat up straighter. "He believes...he believes...*you* have power," she said slowly.

"Earlier this year, my father asked me to help him find the witch descendants because he thought they would have the diary," Evil continued. "This is what came out." She flipped the drawing over and straightened out her arms, the drawing pinned between her thumb and forefinger on either side.

Ms. Goode stood and walked toward the drawing, squinting. "I see a book? No, a notebook. A journal. Some writing in a journal." She gasped. "The Library motto!"

Evil nodded. "We couldn't read what it was. But in two weeks, we got this call that The Library of Strange and Unusual Things was holding a diary that belonged to my father."

Ms. Goode stepped closer, and then a strangling sound rose in her throat.

"Oh God. Oh Ava." She looked at Evil, her lips parted, her hand reaching to cover her mouth.

Evil's mouth quivered. "I knew you could read it. I drew Dr. Hathorne, taking notes on the diary." Her teeth began to chatter. "Some things are real even if you don't believe in them, Ms. Goode."

Evil dropped the drawing and covered her eyes.

"Dr. Hathorne didn't kill Davey's dad. I did."

"No!" Ms. Goode cried, grabbing Evil's hands and pulling them away from her face. "No, you did not do this, Ava!"

Evil shook all over, but the tears would not come. "Yes, I did. I didn't mean to hurt anyone, but I've been hurting people my whole life without meaning to." The faces of classmates she'd drawn when she was upset hurtled through her mind.

I'm bad. I'm horrible. No wonder Davey hates me!

"Ava, listen to me!" Ms. Goode spoke so fast she gulped for air. "Davey's father is a descendant of the accused. He didn't want to participate in the Community. He never told his family, but he agreed to be our protector. He knew everything. Ava, I *asked* him to check on Dr. Hathorne."

"Because my drawing made you do that, Ms. Goode."

"And your father made you draw it!" Ms. Goode kneeled down, her breath weak. "Don't you see? Sometimes, Ava, sometimes accidents just...happen!"

Ms. Goode shook her head and put her hand on her chest. She exhaled and then struggled to inhale again. Evil leaned toward the librarian.

"Ms. Goode...are you okay? What's wrong?"

Ms. Goode gestured toward her bag behind them, on a chair in the dining room. "Inhaler," she croaked out.

Evil helped Ms. Goode to lie down on her bed, and then she ran to the purse. She rummaged until her hands closed on something small and plastic that she quickly gave to Ms. Goode. The librarian puffed on the inhaler. Her eyebrows shot up, and she held up the inhaler and inspected it, her face a mask of surprise. It dropped from her hands, and she wheezed at Evil.

"Get...help," Ms. Goode rasped, with fear in her eyes.

Evil hesitated, gripped by her own terror, and then bolted, yelling as she fled down the hall and into the main floor.

CHAPTER 21—EVIL

The Anniversary

Ms. Goode had fainted by the time the ambulance arrived. Evil only got to squeeze the hand of the librarian once before they put her onto the stretcher and took her away, sirens blaring in the darkness.

I bet it was the diary. I let her read the diary notes. I hurt everyone.

Evil gulped the night air, then stopped short of going up the stairs back into the Library. She turned and stared at the Narnia lamppost to the right of the stairs. She gripped the straps of her backpack as she closed her eyes and imagined Davey sitting on the opposite wall, chin in his hands.

Davey, come back. Come back.

She opened her eyes, shivered, and rubbed her arms, but not because she was cold. She was alone again.

But I don't deserve you, do I, Davey? I hurt people.

A tear ran down Evil's cheek.

There's only one person I deserve.

Her silent words suddenly came back to her.

Be careful! Watch out, he might be anywhere!

He? Who's he?

"It's...Father," she whispered. "I was warning...myself...about Father."

The clock tower bonged six times.

Evil didn't have a name for the feeling welling inside her. She'd only allowed herself to really feel it toward bullies, and then she ended up drawing something horrible about them. Her heart raced and her whole body gradually filled with the heat of it. She balled her hands into fists and stood up, flexing her hands, clenching her jaw.

It's six o'clock on the Anniversary. I will find Father.

Evil turned to the profile of the menacing gargoyle perched beside the staircase and did not feel afraid. She imagined the stone shimmering and melting as she stared at it before racing up the long stone steps.

She gritted her teeth as she entered through the double doors of The Library of Strange and Unusual Things because something had changed. A lot more visitors milled around on the floor than usual, and the air held a charge, some tension, like...like...

Like right before a storm.

Evil ducked behind a big column and tried to reach out with her mind to grab the crackling electricity in the air, to use it to help her.

Help me find Father. I don't want to run from him anymore.

She walked around the column and tried to follow the energy that swirled around the Library. It led her past the main staff area to where a crowd gathered. Evil squirmed through the adults until she reached the front. She shrank back at a life-size display behind the large sign announcing Cotton Mather's diary would be revealed tomorrow.

Under a single soft light, a rail-thin mannequin with dark brown hair stood on a cart. Evil's eyes trailed the familiar dirt streaks on the woman's face, the red patches on her sunken cheeks. Her once-white cap lay on her back; a thin string around her neck kept it from falling off. Her right arm pointed ramrod straight, her upper arm displaying the witch's brand.

Evil followed her pointing finger to another small light from the ceiling, which illuminated her ancestor, Cotton Mather, astride a horse. Just like in her dream. She closed her eyes for longer than a blink and opened them again, taking in the lifelike scene.

Evil pushed her way out of the crowd again, walked a few feet away, and leaned against a wall. She breathed in and out several times before opening her eyes. She looked back at the display, at the accused witch pointing at Cotton. Evil blinked sleepily, letting everything blur as she followed the direction of the woman's pointing finger farther past the display, and that's when she saw it.

A sign stood in front of a set of double doors past the spiral staircase. Flickering light poured from a crack in the doors, tugging at her, urging her toward them as if she had a rope tied to her waist.

Then she stood before the sign: THE TRIAL OF THE 17th CENTURY, OPEN FOR PUBLIC VIEWING OCTOBER 31. *Trial.* She dropped her backpack, not wanting her sketchbook near her, hoping beyond hope she never saw it again, and pulled one of the heavy oak doors open.

She stepped into a courtroom filled with electric candlelight. Plain benches with candles on the ends lined up in front of her, like a church except without the path in the middle. Several people sat quietly on the benches dressed in what looked like pilgrim clothes to Evil, the women in skirts and their heads covered with white caps, the men in short pants that stopped at the knee, tall hats beside them on the benches.

But as Evil watched, fake candlelight moved, but the people didn't. *This has to be another display.*

At the center of the room stood a modest judge's area, stairs on either side of a tall desk that had a gavel resting on its side. Candles glowed on either side of the desk as a man in a gray wig that flowed over his shoulders stared gravely at the witness stand.

A girl stood on the witness stand. Her arms flailed high over her head, her neck arched back, her mouth in the shape of a scream. A stray red hair from under her cap stirred in an unseen breeze. Several men in long black robes stood around, and behind her, some with outstretched arms like they were trying to stop her, hold her. One man merely stood with his hands clasped behind his back, leaning forward, like he was examining her.

"Incredibly lifelike, aren't they?" the examining figure said without turning around.

Her father straightened up and turned toward her. His eyes had large, dark hollows under them, and his face had the beginnings of a beard. He walked to the center of the room, in front of the judge's desk.

Evil struggled to keep the heat coursing through her veins, the courage that led her to find him.

"I knew I didn't need to tell you how to find me on the Anniversary. Just like you found me before, in the basement. That's because I know you so very, very well."

He smiled and lines sprouted across his face. His bloodshot eyes bore into hers.

"I apologize for my absence, but I was determined to keep my promise to read the diary by the Anniversary. The antiquarian was remarkably compliant. In restoring the diary, he removed all of the pages from the binding and allowed me to read each one that he restored, as long as I promised not to touch it. It was extremely time-consuming, and I could not be disturbed." He smiled again, and the candlelight flashed on his forehead, shiny with sweat. "You understand. It's all for you. And you've waited long enough for this most precious of heirlooms." Her father gestured to something in front of him.

Evil eased her way toward the front of the room until a small table came into view. It held a large, single sheet of paper with two pencils. A small chair on the side faced the people on the benches.

Before the paper sat an old-fashioned mirror on a golden stand right beside...

The diary. It has to be.

Long and black, with curly silver writing on the cover.

He does have it. Father always gets his way.

"You read it," Evil whispered, shocked. "You read the...whole diary."

"It's time to be cured, Evil." He gave a small laugh. "How wonderful it will be to never call you that name again." He held out his arms to her.

Tears sprang to her eyes, and the heat drained from her limbs. What had he read? She only heard some notes. He'd read the whole diary. What else was in there?

Evil edged toward her father, hugging the benches, touching each one as she passed it.

"I understand you're both excited and scared. We've talked about this for a long time. You are probably having a hard time believing this isn't a dream."

The display of Sarah Goode pointing at Cotton flashed in her mind. She swallowed as she reached the end of the benches.

"Father, what did you find in the diary?"

He smiled again. "Of course, I am happy to tell you everything." He gestured to the paper. "After your final drawing."

Her mouth dropped open. "You said...you said when I was cured you would...I would never have to draw again! It would be my choice!"

"Your final drawing *is* the cure." He touched his crest and nodded. "This is your final trial."

Evil's stomach clenched. She turned, scanning the faces of the people on the benches as if they could help her. Their glassy eyes stared at the woman on the witness stand.

I can't do it! I won't hurt someone else!

The Reverend strode to her and took her hand, but Evil snatched it away. Shaking, she took several steps backward.

"You...you can't make me. You can't make me draw anything."

He smiled sadly at her. "Have I ever *made* you draw anything, Evil? Tied you to a chair?"

Evil looked away. No, he hadn't forced her, but...she had trusted him. Trusted that he knew best. Now she couldn't trust him at all.

Maybe...maybe that's why she really had to come here. To tell him she knew what he really was: a liar.

She turned toward him and opened her mouth, but the words wouldn't come.

The Reverend gestured to the table. "Are you really going to throw away what you've waited for your whole life? I thought you wanted to be normal, Evil. I'm giving you that opportunity, just like I promised."

Evil's eyes slid from the paper to the mirror and then stopped. A mirror. A mirror. She whipped around to face her father.

"You...you want me to draw MYSELF!" Her voice echoed in the courtroom. She glanced from the mirror to her father, who held his sad smile. "You said to never draw you and never draw myself! Ever!"

He clasped his hands together. "I never dreamt the diary would guide us in this way, Evil, it's the last—"

"No." It came out as a whisper because she'd never refused to draw for him. She glanced at the mirror again and shook her head as she eyed her father.

He suddenly rushed at her, grabbed her arms, shook her. Evil gasped, too stunned to speak.

"Do you know what it's like to raise a child who can hurt people? Do you? I've lived my life protecting others from you, even as the Mathers died around me!"

Evil found her voice, tried to scream at him, but it came out scratchy, her voice breaking. "But you never protected ME!"

His eyes bore into hers. "I spent my life searching for a cure. What else could you possibly ask of me?"

"You should have believed I wasn't completely bad!"

He dropped his hands from her arms and took a step back. His hand slipped into his robes. "As I said, I have never forced you to draw anything."

He gently withdrew a statue of Davey and sat it on the table. She stared at Davey's face, a mournful, suffering look.

"I know you would never make me hurt Davey."

Her head snapped up.

"You can't," she said, her lower lip trembling. "It's just a statue...it's just a stupid...statue!" But her heart beat louder and louder in her ears.

He scooped up the Davey statue and held it to his chest, both hands wrapped around it. "Is it, Evil? Is that what the witches said? I'm trying to help you make the right decision. Won't you help yourself?" Then he held the Davey statue high over his head. "Would you risk Davey's life because you've decided I'm untrustworthy?"

Despite everything she wanted to believe, Evil's throat swelled and her eyes fixed on the Davey statue held in the air.

Don't drop it, don't drop it, please don't drop it, don't...

"Lies," Evil choked out, clawing at her throat, agonizing over the suspended statue. "You've only lied to me."

"Lying to protect a child from understanding the depth of her capacity to harm? That makes me a horrible man? Does that also make me a liar right now?" He slowly let the Davey statue slip a little from his grasp.

Evil screamed and bolted forward, and he grabbed her wrist with lightning speed, a ferocity she'd never known. His grip increased and he pulled her down to her knees.

Tears dribbled from her eyes. To her surprise, his eyes filled with tears too.

"It's your choice, Evil," he whispered. "But I will do everything in my power to make sure you are cured. Even if it means threatening this poor boy's life." He sighed and blinked, a single tear rolling down his cheek. "Please. Don't make me do this."

Evil went limp, and he slipped the statue back into his robes as he picked her up in his arms like a rag doll.

"Trust me, Evil, trust me."

He softly placed her into the chair at the table. The Reverend pulled her into a sitting position and placed his hands on her shoulders.

Evil struggled to get air into her lungs. The Reverend squeezed her shoulders like he used to. He leaned over the table to adjust the golden mirror until Evil gazed at her own frightened face.

"Now, concentrate, Evil." She heard his usual intake of breath before he started guiding her with his voice into a drawing. Evil's nails dug into the table. He wouldn't speak until she picked up the pencils.

She stared at the diary, nausea washing over her. It was glossier close up, like it had been polished...

Ms. Goode's voice echoed in her head. *It mimics leather well, at a distance.*

Her hand shot out, and her father squeezed her shoulder painfully.

"It's fake," she said out loud, touching the diary. "It's wood. You haven't read the diary!"

Gradually the Reverend's grip on her shoulders relaxed, and his hands released her. Evil turned. Tears ran down his face. When he spoke, his voice creaked with sadness.

"No, Evil. I have read the diary." He paused for a long time. "I'm the one who sent it to the Library."

Evil stared. And stared. More tears ran down the Reverend's face.

"The diary was never lost. It's been...protected by the Clan. For a long time. It took years of study and consultation with the Mather Clan to understand the Curse after you were born."

Evil turned away and stared dully into the mirror, not seeing herself, not seeing anything.

"Because after you were born, we lost our special gift." In the mirror, her father held the Davey statue and gazed at it. "For a long time."

Gift? Cotton's gift?

He put the Davey statue down with a small clink. "You are the thief who stole the gift from the Mathers, whether you meant to or not."

The memory of her father's tears, the statues of her, the accusations that she was a thief, and Ms. Goode saying how everything had changed since she was born fell together. Understanding hit her in the chest, winding her. *So that's why I had to stay in my room on the Anniversary...that's why the Mathers hate me...*

"We had to discover why. Everyone suspected the Curse. And the more we studied the diary, the more we agreed that was indeed the case."

Evil looked at the blank sheet of paper. That's how she felt. Blank. Blank. Blank.

"I told you not to draw yourself because I thought I could save you from being evil. But I couldn't. The Clan and I tried to regain the gift, but we couldn't get it back, not then, not for many years. And many didn't want to face life without it."

That's why they've been dying...

Evil watched her father's face in the mirror. "But the Curse...Virtue...you brought me here."

"Yes. The irony of appearing as if we are fulfilling the Goode Curse instead of ending it. It took years, but you helped us find the descendants, slowly, with your drawings."

My drawings?

"We could only eliminate descendants as we stumbled upon them, but your power..." He shook his head, closing his eyes briefly. "Your power reduced their number and ultimately led us to the secret witches' lair where so many descendants fled hundreds of years ago. I just had to get you to believe in the diary and determine, over time, the right questions to ask you so I could find them. Your drawing told me where they were, and where to finally send the diary."

He sighed. "Dr. Hathorne's death was...unfortunate. An unintended sacrifice to the cause."

What does he mean?

"Under no other circumstances would the descendants ever allow a Mather inside the Library. But they could not resist the diary, something I could legally claim, something I knew they wanted as much as you did. But it won't do them any good." His voice grew hoarse. "I can renew Cotton's mission on this Anniversary. A new beginning for the Clan."

Evil squinted at her father's reflection, struggling to comprehend everything, her mind sluggish and sticky with overwhelming despair.

"There's no cure," Evil whispered. "The diary never had a cure."

He raised his eyes to the ceiling. "You will be cured, Evil. It's not the cure you want, it's not from the diary, but it is a cure. The only one I have discovered in twelve years." His voice broke. "And if you don't obey me this one last time, Davey will suffer the consequences."

One last time...one last time? What does he mean?

"The Davey statue...the statue doesn't work," Evil whispered.

"Sarah Goode was not the only prophet, Evil. Cotton was as well. The moment we arrived in Virtue, things began to change. Why do you think I began making statues again? And things are already coming to pass: You don't think Ms. Goode fell ill by accident, do you?"

He pulled a statue of Ms. Goode from his other pocket to show her, then returned it to his robes. "And once the Curse is completely lifted, our gifts will be fully restored to all of us."

He settled his hands on her shoulders again. "We've waited for twelve years. Let us lift it at last."

Us? You and me? Or...you and the Clan?

"Don't worry," the Reverend said in a gentle tone. "You won't remember any of this after you're cured."

Cured. Evil didn't move. She continued to focus on the mirror.

Everything grew still and quiet in her heart.

She considered her pale skin, her freckles, her crazy hair. She hated that face.

She watched her hands pick up the pencils.

"Evil has suffered for too long," her father said. "Friendless."

Evil's hands gripped the pencils.

"Motherless."

She held her breath, resisting the pull to the paper.

"Isolated."

She bit her tongue to the point of blood.

"She cries in her room when she thinks her father doesn't hear her."

Evil's reflection quivered, whether because she shook with the effort of resisting the sketch pad or her eyes were blurred with tears, she wasn't sure.

"When her classmates hurt her, she hurts them back in her drawings. Whether she intends to or not. Hurting others is in her nature. It always has been."

Evil didn't blink.

"She wounds children without meaning to. She hurts everyone. She does not want to be what she is. Sin will always triumph." He paused. "How can we end Evil's suffering?"

She hated Evil. She had always hated her. Evil didn't have friends. Evil hurt people. She just wanted to be...

"How can we end Evil's pain?"

Ava. That's who she wanted to be. Ava. Ava had friends. Ava tried to help people.

Her eyes closed, her own image staining the backs of her eyelids as her father spoke. Her fingers grasped the pencils. When her hands began to move across the page, the light wavered outside her eyelids. Words skittered across her mind before disintegrating like chalk dust against the darkness...

I don't want to be Evil anymore.

I don't like her.

I hate her.

Memories of red paint splashed on her coat, finding disgusting things in her school lunches, sitting alone, always alone, and other childhood tortures floated through her mind.

But then the recent memory of the Reverend's words stabbed through these thoughts.

I found the descendants at last...

Descendant. Descendant? Another memory floated up from when she eavesdropped on his calls in his study.

"I have found one on the list. The actual descendant. Good."

Good. Good.

Goode?

Could he...did he mean Ms. Goode?

Your power led us to the secret witches' lair...

Witches...the accused...the Community?

Then she heard the echo of another memory—her father's voice again, speaking about Ms. Goode:

An adult who conducts business through children is not to be trusted...

A ball of flames burst in Evil's chest. Lightning rushed throughout her limbs, her neck, her face, to the ends of her hair. She gripped the pencils, pressing down hard until something warm and sticky seeped under her hands. Warmth radiated from her palms, up her arms, spreading like a hot, swirling aura around her. Then her hands began to move, and she couldn't hear her father's voice anymore. Just her own, in her head. And another voice, a woman's, one she had only heard in her dreams, chorused with her, chanting something familiar with Evil until her voice rose to a scream...

But it was the Reverend's screams that brought her out of her trance. Her eyes snapped open, and the reflection in the mirror was not hers but her father's anguished face, wavering in the candlelight.

She wheeled around to see her father holding his hands up to his face.

She could faintly see his frightened eyes through his palms, as if, as if...

Evil gasped in horror. She stood back from the Reverend.

The Reverend threw his hands down to face her. The walls behind him began to show through his robes like he was a movie, an image against the walls.

He was fading. Becoming a watercolor version of himself.

Shaking, Evil stepped away as the Reverend moved toward her, his entire form growing fainter by the second.

"Evil."

His voice came out hollow and full of echoes. He took another step, his face contorting like it hurt him to move.

"You don't know...what else I've done."

Evil edged backward. His image flickered and wavered like the candlelight.

"There are many ways...to fulfill...Cotton's mission." Now it was only the sound of rustling leaves.

He leaned forward, reaching out a shaking hand, a pale shadow dissolving in the light.

"Without me, your power will...consume...everyone."

Then the Reverend mouthed her name, but she couldn't hear him.

And as she peered into his wide, quivering eyes, she was suddenly staring at nothing but the statues of Davey and Ms. Goode rolling on the floor.

CHAPTER 22—DAVEY

103 days since the accident

Davey sat in front of the TV set with his ma, but he had no idea what they were watching. He couldn't stop replaying what had happened at the Library. The look on Ava's face. The look on Ms. Goode's face. But worst of all, he'd told Ava how he really felt.

Something he should never have thought, much less said out loud.

Ava, who had no ma to comfort her. Ava, whose father seemed...well, scary. Scary.

And a liar.

"Davey! Why are you crying?" His ma turned off the TV. Only the little table lamp lit the room. She pulled Davey into her soft arms, and then the waterworks really started to flow. His ma pulled out a box of tissues, and Davey blew his nose. Crying was bad enough, but he hated how it made his nose run on top of everything else.

"Would it make you feel better to talk about it?"

"Yeah...I think." Guilt made his heart thump when her face lit up. "Ma, do you think there are things that are, um, unforgivable? Like, something a friend could do that would make you not want to be their friend anymore?"

His ma raised her eyebrows and tilted her head to one side. "I suppose so. I mean, if anyone ever hurt you, I don't know if I could forgive them. Hurt you on purpose, I mean, of course. And, maybe if someone intentionally hurt any child or animal or something innocent like that." She touched the gold cross around her neck. "I suppose that's not terribly Christian of me. And I want to be honest with you that it is always best to forgive if you can."

Davey sat cuddled in his mother's arm. *Forgive...*

Was it just that he needed Ava to forgive him? No, there was something else. Something that just kept coming up, kept bothering him, upsetting him.

I need to forgive Ava for not being normal. His insides squeezed tight, but he forced himself to face it: *And for sometimes reminding me that I don't feel normal either.*

His face grew hot, and he worried he might cry again. Her father might be a liar, but he had touched something Davey hadn't realized he wanted to protect when he talked about a broken child.

Davey took in a shaky breath, the hurt in Ava's eyes fresh in his mind. *I can't blame her for what happened to my dad. It's not fair.*

"Do you think you could forgive someone who hurt something...or someone...by accident?"

"I would try," his ma said, nodding. "I would try very hard." His mother hugged him and then gave him a sidelong glance. "But, Davey, someone would have to *ask* me for forgiveness first."

She stood, and Davey looked up, puzzled. "It's late, but it's a Saturday. I will drive you to the Library, and you can just call me after you've apologized for whatever you've said to that girl, okay?"

Davey's jaw dropped, and she pulled her chin into her neck and raised one eyebrow.

"Davey, that's the only place you ever go other than school. I assume she must live pretty close to the Library."

Davey swallowed, then licked his lips.

"Ma? Would you mind...if I invited her over for dinner sometime?"

At the Library, Davey tried the door to Ava's quarters, but it was locked. His heart thudded at the thought of running into the Reverend, but he had to find her. He had to find her. Then a thought stilled him.

What if she's gone?

What if her father took her away?

What if the Reverend found out that they'd met again?

What if—

Davey's heart boomed in his ears, and his back grew hot under his backpack, which he'd grabbed out of sheer habit on the way out. While he didn't *want* to believe what the Reverend had told him about Ava, it only now dawned on him that he could put her in danger just by being with her. Because of her dad.

But would that have stopped me?

Guilt wrapped around Davey like a scratchy wool blanket in summer. Davey frowned and squirmed, hunching his shoulders and stuffing his hands in his pockets. At the same time, the thought of Ava tugged at him, pulled him along, humming *find me, find me, Davey.*

He couldn't believe he was bad for her. Her father was bad for her but not him.

No, it wouldn't have stopped me. And it's not going to stop me now.

He walked away from her door, sliding down behind a large column where no one could see him. He had to think. What had they learned from the diary? That would probably help him find her now. He ticked his thoughts off on his fingers.

1. Her great-great-great-grandfather made statues he thought gave him some temporary mind control over people.
2. Sarah Goode cursed Cotton because she knew Cotton's secret—the statues.
3. Cotton thought the curse was why his daughter died and that the way to end it was to kill witches so no more curses could happen.

Davey briefly put his head on his knees, ashamed of what he had said all over again. So how did this all add up to finding Ava? She seemed to still think she was cursed. And would be forever.

Wait. The cure. The Anniversary. *No. No, it ...it's tonight!* Then her father would be looking for her. Might have found her. Davey's mind pulsed with panic.

How much did he know? What would he do to Ava? Would he...

A thought so terrible leapt into his mind that he raced to the front desk and pounded on it to get Barton's attention.

"Okay, gosh, we're a library, not a bar. What do you need?" Barton sighed, annoyed, walking over from his small desk.

"How"—Davey gasped, fighting to slow his heart down—"would you get to the towers?"

"Well, they're only open on certain occasions, and now they're under construction—"

"But how would I get to them then?" Davey asked, gripping the desk.

"Don't—you're gonna scar it." Barton waved at Davey's hands, and Davey released his grip. "When they're not under construction, you take the corner stairwell at each of the four ends of the main floor. Geesh."

"Four spires, four floors," Davey said, and Barton nodded.

"Hey," he said sharply. "You know the public isn't allowed up there, so why are you asking?"

Davey hesitated, and then relief flooded him. He dug into the front pocket of his backpack and placed his Treasure Hunt prize, the sealed scroll, on the desk.

"One isn't under construction. A librarian is waiting to guide me on the tour of the spire mentioned there, a tour I won last year fair and square. So that's why I'm asking."

Barton raised his chin and with a wary look felt beneath the desk, emerging with a letter opener that he used to break the seal. When he unrolled it, his face fell as he read it. Then he gave Davey a cool look.

"*Which* librarian?"

Davey stared at Barton for a moment.

"Mrs...Smmmmiiith?"

Barton shrugged and waved the scroll at Davey.

"Go ahead then."

Davey nodded and exhaled. "Thanks, Barton." He made a mental note to seek out whoever Mrs. Smith was the next time he was at the Library.

He fast-walked until he got to the far-left back corner. And there was a really narrow stairwell with an Under Construction sign, but Davey didn't care. He tried the knob, and it gave under his hand. He flung open the door.

To stare at a pile of rubble.

"Oh, he wasn't kidding," Davey mumbled to himself.

The next stairwell was locked, and the next one had a huge pile of desks, chairs, and other furniture blocking the entrance.

"Geez!" Davey said aloud, turning around and stomping away.

He took a deep breath and made his way to the final stairwell. It had no sign that it was under construction—a hunch on Davey's part that paid off. Davey tried the handle and it opened easily. He peered inside. The electric candle winked in its hole in the wall. The stairs looked completely sturdy.

But they sure hurt by the thirteenth floor, which led into the spire. His lungs complained and he leaned on his knees a moment. When he stood up, he faced a small wooden door. He turned the black handle and then clung to it because the wind nearly flung the door against the wall. He caught it before it hit and pulled it shut behind him with some effort.

From afar, the towers had always looked just like the ones in fairy tales, but he hadn't known how close they were to the real thing. Only bare stone and glassless windows cut into the walls surrounded him in this tiny, drafty tower. And it was empty—nothing could hide behind anything here. He crept toward a window and looked out.

The wall shot way down, and the wind whipped his hair as he stared in awe at the lawn and little people walking around. The fog made everything blurry, and for a second, everyone looked like Cotton's "miniatures" come to life. Davey gulped down his nausea. He strained and squinted and pushed his body as far as it could safely go out of the window. Thankfully, everything looked normal. No one was crowded around anything that had fallen...or been pushed. He briefly shut his eyes and shook his head, trying to rid himself of the image he'd had earlier of the Reverend pushing Ava out of the tower, her long curls flying...

He pulled himself back inside the spire and slid down the cold wall.

And no one was being hidden here, either.

Davey tried not to think of the poem that had inspired Ava's name. She wasn't lost, she wasn't. She couldn't be. The clock tower bonged, and to Davey, it sounded like it was calling for her, looking for Ava.

The outside lights suddenly dimmed and then brightened. The wind made a crying sound as it blew fiercely through the windows, and Davey shivered, wrapping his arms around himself. But as the wind died down, the crying became clearer.

Davey perked up his ears and swiveled his head. Where was it coming from? It sounded like something in the floor... He crawled around on his hands and knees in the dark tower, and the crying sound got louder when he stumbled upon a vent that blended with the dark stone. He pressed his ear to the cold slats.

Somebody was definitely crying. It was really faint but it was there.

Davey stood, flung the door open, and shut it firmly before he took the stone steps down as fast as he could to the next landing: the twelfth floor. He found the vent closest to where he'd been in the tower.

It was still somewhere below, still super weak.

Davey went floor by floor, searching and listening at vents. The crying began to get louder the lower he went. Finally, he was back on the first floor, staring at the vastness of the main level. Puzzled, he made his way to the front.

A few tourists lingered around some display. Davey approached it and gasped at the sight of the rail-thin woman pointing at the man on the horse. *Ava's drawing.*

But Davey's eyes followed the woman's pointing finger past the man on the horse. Davey half turned and his eyes trailed the opposite wall until they landed on Ava's backpack.

Davey exhaled in a rush as he ran across the Library floor to kneel in front of the dirty aqua backpack. He picked it up.

He looked up and realized it wasn't just a wall but two large double doors right in front of him. How could he miss something like this? And one of the doors stood ajar...

Slinging Ava's backpack over the shoulder opposite his own backpack, he cautiously approached and peeked inside.

Davey blinked, taken aback by the flickering candles and people on the benches. Ava sat at the front of a courtroom with her face in her hands, sobbing. The crying he'd heard all the way up in the tower.

She's alive. I found the treasure.

He rushed around the benches until he reached her, sitting at a little table.

"Ava!" he cried.

She dropped her hands from her face and leapt into his arms, still weeping. His shirt got wet real fast. For a while, only her choking sobs filled the courtroom.

Then she pulled back from him.

"What happened?" he asked, raising his voice in concern at her blood-smeared face.

"How...how did you know where I was?" she sputtered.

"You left your backpack outside."

She shook her head. "You can't stay. You can't stay." The tears turned into red trails.

"But, but I just got here!" he cried, anxious to make everything right. "And I've got something important to tell you."

She backed away, shaking her head.

"I'm sorry, I felt so awful I just had to hug you, but now you really need to leave."

"Ava, what happened? You have blood all over your face. Are you okay?"

Ava lifted her hands and gasped. Globs of blood stained her fingers and palms.

What's she done? What's she done? He couldn't help staring at her bloody hands.

"I don't...I...he told me I had to draw myself," she finally choked out. "Davey, my whole life, my whole life he said never to draw myself. But he threatened you..."

"What? How?" Davey asked, bewildered.

Ava picked up the Davey statue from the table and showed it to him.

His eyes widened and then he looked at something else on the table. "Whoa. Is that...is that Ms. Goode?" He looked at Ava. "But I thought they didn't work anymore!"

Ava nodded, gasping through her tears. "I don't know...I just don't know what would happen if he broke it. I didn't want to take the chance! So I actually tried to draw myself. I thought...I thought..."

She sat the Davey statue down on the table. "He said he wanted Evil to go away, and I wanted her...me...to go away too." She closed her eyes and her throat contracted. "But when I let myself go, when I let drawing take over, this is what I drew." Her voice broke as she pointed at the piece of paper on the table, but Davey didn't want to look. He just wanted to help her.

"Ava," he began, an uneasy feeling stealing into his gut. "Where's your dad?"

She raised her head and shook it slowly, her lips trembling.

"He thought...he thought he could outsmart the Curse, Davey. I didn't mean to...I mean, I didn't plan...but it came true anyway. I think I...did end...the Mather line."

He glanced again at her hands. "Ava, did you...is your dad hurt?"

"I don't know," she whispered, not looking at him. "Davey, he was lying about so many things, but he was right about me. I'm bad. I'm wrong! You've got to leave, you've got to!"

"Ava!" He stepped close to her. "Ava, *I* was wrong. I was wrong to not show up that day. And I was wrong to ask you to help...about my dad." His heart beat faster as he found himself wondering where her dad was.

Her breathing slowed. "I know what you want. I know you want your father to be alive again. And you want me to try to do that."

Yes.

He shook his head violently. "No. No! It's wrong. It was wrong of me to think it, much less say it."

"But I understand, Davey. I do. And I want to try to give it to you. I owe you that."

His insides chilled. "No. Don't even. You don't owe me anything."

"I want to try. But you can't stay while I do it."

He tried a different approach. "Then it's not right. If I can't stay, it's not right. Whatever you're thinking."

She pleaded with him. "Please? Please? Won't you let me try to make it up to you?"

"Make what up to me?"

Her mouth opened and closed without sound again. She lowered her head and shook it sadly.

"I'm not good for you, Davey. I'm not." Her hands dropped and her shoulders sagged.

He sensed she was slipping into something dangerous, someplace he wouldn't be able to reach her.

His eyes flicked to the paper and back to Ava. "Did you...did you want to hurt him when you were drawing?"

She lowered her tear-stained face and shook her head. "It's hard to remember, Davey, I was so scared...and I had so many voices in my head..."

Voices? She's hearing voices?

Davey breathed in and out several times. "Then don't assume you've done anything wrong."

"But he's gone!"

"He is?"

Ava nodded.

"But we don't know he's hurt, right?"

Ava hesitated before shaking her head.

Davey swallowed. "And, uh, you can't...you know...undo whatever...happened." He glanced at the paper on the table again.

Her lips parted in shock. "But you said...about your dad..."

Davey shook his head, his lips pressed firmly together. "That's different, Ava. We know what happened to my dad. There's no...assuming. We know."

Her voice got quiet. "I don't know how to undo what I draw, Davey. I was...going to try something new to...for you."

Davey didn't speak right away. "Draw something...good?"

Her lips trembled, the red streaks drying on her cheeks. "I wanted to try."

"Ava." Davey spoke quietly too, his eyes flicking between the frozen audience and the paper on the table. "Ava, trying is everything. I mean,

I don't want you to do anything about my dad, but...yeah, I really think you should try to draw something good."

Ava stared, her eyes sad.

"You won't be alone. We can experiment. So we'll figure out what you can...and can't...do. So then we'll know. Right?"

"Know what?" Ava asked in a small voice.

"That you can make good things happen too."

Her eyes widened.

"We can start small, Ava."

"Davey, I don't know if I can do small."

"We'll be careful. Real careful. But you can't live like this, Ava. No one could. Not knowing?"

Ava looked at the paper on the table. "I don't want to hurt anybody, Davey."

Davey reached out and touched her left hand. "Then let's figure it out. As best we can."

This time Davey hugged Ava, for a long time.

As his arms encircled Ava, Davey stared at the witness stand, the young girl's tortured face. He closed his eyes and prayed he was doing the right thing. When he opened them, his gaze fell on the paper sitting on the table, right near him. Close enough to see what was on it.

Nausea rose in Davey's throat.

The robes and crest around the neck in the picture made it look like the Reverend. But in the sketch, his hands reached toward a face that wasn't there. The rest of him dripped like a melting candle, as if he wasn't going to be a man much longer.

And the entire drawing was in blood.

CHAPTER 23—DAVEY

E *arly December*

Davey regretted not taking Ms. Goode's offer to drive him up to her house. Most places in Virtue took about fifteen minutes to walk to, but this had taken him almost an hour. As he panted, dragging himself up the drive, he corrected himself: mansion, not house. Ms. Goode's mansion. Six stories with things she called *turrets* on the sides and a balcony and everything. The stone had a purple hue that made Davey think of the Disneyland castle. A small version of it, but still. All this time and he never knew she was the owner of the mansion on the hill. The librarian said she'd inherited it and had to take in boarders to keep it up. She limited the boarders to her Community so they could talk freely at any time like they could in that room in the Library.

He used both hands to pick up the big, brassy door knocker, which a golden lion clenched in its jaws, and let it drop. The *BOOM* that followed impressed him. And sure enough, Ms. Goode opened the door not much later.

Davey did a double take because Ms. Goode looked so different with her hair loose. She looked so different when she smiled, too. She wore jeans that flared at the bottom with boots and a turtleneck that reminded him more of high schoolers than a librarian.

"Thank you for coming so soon, Davey, she'll be so glad to see you."

He gaped as he entered a wide hall with towering arched ceilings, columns, and large portraits on either side.

"The Community used to have a lot more money. My distant relatives had a huge gold mining operation here," Ms. Goode explained.

"Yeah?" Davey asked, in awe of the place, looking at the slick tiled floor.

"Actually, let me show you something." Ms. Goode gestured to follow her through an archway. After they walked through a small hall and an enormous kitchen, they entered an adjoining spacious room with windows on every side and a small table in a corner. It looked like a breakfast nook to Davey. His mom had always wanted one. Even standing in the archway to the room, Davey could see snow-capped mountains surrounding them.

"So my commute is not great, but this is," Ms. Goode said, gesturing to the view.

"Yeah!" Davey agreed, gawking, wanting to walk on the clouds.

He turned to the librarian. "Ms. Goode, is Ava going to live with you...well, forever?"

Her smile faded.

"Until her father is found. The investigation is ongoing. I'm her closest living relative, and she won't become a ward of the state as long as I am here."

Davey squirmed, still adjusting to the fact that Ava and Ms. Goode were related. But a *ward*? Davey didn't like the sound of that. And Ms. Goode had to be a much better parent than the Reverend. Actually, a slug was probably a better parent than the Reverend.

"Did, uh...did Ava tell you what happened?" he asked cautiously.

"Yes. And I find it as strange as you do."

Davey leaned toward her. "You do?"

Ms. Goode nodded gravely. "To have come all this way for the diary, dragging his daughter across the continent, only to abandon her like that? It doesn't make any sense."

"You think he's, uh, hiding or something?" Davey asked, wondering what Ava had told her.

"I just know he's not here in Virtue," Ms. Goode said, sighing. "And he left everything behind, including dozens of clay figures."

"Like the one of me?" Davey asked, his eyebrows high.

Ms. Goode nodded. "Yes. All members of the Community—myself included." She covered her face with her hands for a moment and then dropped them. "Ava was worth it, but I will always live with the guilt of letting a Mather into our Library, toothless as I believed him to be at this point."

"How come you let him live there, Ms. Goode?"

"We wanted access to Ava. And we extracted a small fortune to allow him in." She paused. "We tried to restrict his movement by posting those signs in the stairwells."

Davey's eyes popped. "Ohhhhh..."

"They searched his Boston home and found figures...clay dolls...of my sister and more of my mother," Ms. Goode continued. "A journal full of names that corresponded to the figures, too. Like Cotton, I think he believed in that so-called gift."

"Your mom and sister?" Davey cocked his head to one side. "So the statues *can* do things?" He shuddered.

Ms. Goode's eyes shone as she looked at Davey. "The Mathers would like us to think so. My mother died before Ava was born and my sister during her birth. When Ava was born, Community members stopped dying unnaturally. But given the new statues he made, her father clearly thought his gift wasn't completely gone." She placed her hand on her chest and took a deep breath, then exhaled slowly. Her hand dropped to her side again.

Davey's eyes moved to the hand that she had put on her chest. "Uh, are you feeling okay these days?"

"Having a full inhaler helps greatly." She offered the hint of a smile.

"So you don't think it was...you know," Davey hedged.

"The diary? The statues? No, Davey. I don't."

Davey wasn't so sure. Ms. Goode hadn't seen the indestructible Johnny-drawing. Maybe if you were a Mather, you could do strange stuff.

Ms. Goode cleared her throat and squared her shoulders. "But let me show you where Ava is."

The librarian led him back out of the kitchen, though Davey kept looking behind him at the view, surprised she cut off the conversation so suddenly.

"Uh, Ms. Goode? I noticed all the signs for the diary went away a while back. What happened?"

Ms. Goode's jaw tightened. "It seems to have disappeared, along with the antiquarian I had hired."

"No way!"

"I know. I'm sick about it." She hesitated. "Dr. Hathorne's journal is missing as well."

As shocked as he was, part of him relaxed at the thought that all these things, these *bad* things, might be gone forever.

"But why would someone steal them, Ms. Goode?"

"For one, it keeps us from writing anything about the diary. We couldn't prove anything we said." She paused. "I didn't anticipate this. I hope I didn't underestimate the reverend."

Davey wasn't sure what she meant by the last thing she said, but something else was bugging him.

"Do you think the diary had any answers for Ava? I mean, we just got some notes."

They moved back into the main hall with the portraits and toward a large staircase.

"We have learned something significant about the past, but I don't think a man like Cotton would have any answers for Ava."

They walked up the burgundy-carpeted stairs and came to the landing. A small hallway led to several rooms on either side. Ms. Goode led him to the room at the end.

Ms. Goode knocked softly. "Ava? Davey's here."

After a moment, the knob made a clicking sound, and Davey realized she was unlocking it. Then the knob turned, and Ava peered out from the crack. She eyed both of them and opened the door just wide enough for Davey to slip through.

"Thank you...Aunt Julia," Ava said through the crack in the door once Davey was inside.

"Dinner's at six for...everyone." Ms. Goode laughed a little, and Davey thought it sounded funny. "But we can eat supper privately in the kitchen. Davey, if you want to stay, you're most welcome to."

Ava whipped her head toward Davey behind her and nodded furiously.

"Um, sure, thank you...Ms....Julia. I'll just have to call my ma and make sure it's okay."

Ms. Goode nodded and withdrew while Ava closed the door and then leaned against it.

"Whew," she sighed.

Davey struggled for words as he took in Ava wearing a white dress that just reached her knees. A *dress*. It looked like layers of lace to Davey. With Ava's skin, the dress made her look like a ghostly angel of sorts. Her hair was still really full but softer and her feet were bare. He couldn't stop staring.

"You don't look like you."

Ava's face reddened. "I was just trying this on. For fun."

"No, uh, it looks...you look," Davey stuttered, and then he settled his eyes on her bedroom door instead. "Um, how come you wanted to close your door?"

"I just, uh, I'm really not used to having someone around so much. My—" She stopped. "It's weird having someone ask if I'm okay or hungry all the time. I had nannies who used to make food at certain times, and then I just fed myself when I was older."

"That's what moms do," Davey said, then winced. "That came out wrong. I know she's not your mom."

"It's okay. She's an aunt. That's close." Ava threw her arms out. "Sit wherever you want."

Davey turned. This was no kid's room.

The pale walls went so high Davey had to crane his neck. The ceilings had twisted ropes sculpted into them that crisscrossed and then trailed down the corners of each wall. Purple velvet chairs sat on either side of the room. In the middle was an enormous bed with fancy white and violet trim hanging all around it. But best of all: a huge window that bowed out and held a curved, velvety bench where Ava could sit and look at the mountains.

"Did you find the hedgehog?"

Davey blinked and turned to Ava. "Huh?"

"On the ceiling." She pointed, and he followed her finger until he located a carved hedgehog huddled on one section of rope behind him.

"Ava, this is, uh, this is...wow." Davey kept turning around and gazing appreciatively.

"I know. And no drawings on the wall. And a real bed." She trotted over and bounced on it with a grin.

"You still...have your drawings?"

Ava looked down at her feet and nodded.

"Have you drawn anything since...uh?" He didn't know what to say. *Since your dad disappeared?* It sounded too spooky.

Still looking at her feet, she shrugged.

"Um, do you...wanna talk about your...dad?"

She shook her head again.

"I hate to ask, but what did you do with that statue of me?"

"The police took all of them." Her face darkened, then she looked up and smiled. "Let's talk about something else. Like...what you think about the junior high here. Aunt Julia said I might go there next year."

Davey's heart thudded painfully. That was the last thing he wanted to talk about.

"It's okay. I mean, I've only done a tour and...it's still school. So you're not gonna go to school 'til then?"

"She said she might tutor me for a while instead." Ava paused. "I always wanted that."

Davey tried not to remember that her father had said the tutors never stayed more than a day. *He's a liar. A liar.*

"Oh, you know what? I saw Johnny the other day." Davey grinned weakly, hoping this was not dangerous territory. "He looked rough, but best of all, he went the other way when he saw me."

Ava stayed quiet for a while. Then she said, "That's good. Thanks for telling me."

Davey swallowed. "Um, so, when do you want to start experimenting? You know, drawing some good things? Small things?"

She slid off the bed and opened her closet. "Do you want to see the other new outfits Ms...I mean, Aunt Julia bought me? I can try them on."

Was this the new Ava?

He tried once more to reach the girl he knew. "Ava, you don't believe Ms. Goode's take on all this, do you? That nothing happened? That your drawings can't...that the statues never—" But to his shock, Ava cut him off without turning around.

"I'll just be a few minutes and then come downstairs. Okay?"

He backed out of the room, but then her hand grabbed the door, and she pressed her face to the opening.

"I wanted you to know. I've stopped having that dream. The one I've been having my whole life."

Davey's eyes popped. "For real? When did that happen?"

"Ever since the Anniversary."

She withdrew and softly closed the door.

Davey stood there a moment, unsure of what to think. Then it hit him as he relived Ava crying about what her father had asked her to do: Maybe Ava's drawing really had worked. Maybe "Evil" really had gone away.

He found Ms. Goode in the kitchen. She had a mixing bowl and all sorts of containers around her.

"Ms. Goode? Do you mind if I use your phone?"

Ms. Goode turned with a smile that warmed him. "Of course not, Davey. It's right there on the wall. Help yourself. Your mom and I know each other from church, so I can't imagine she'll mind."

I didn't know that. Huh.

Davey walked over to the phone near the entryway and stopped. He turned back to the librarian.

"Do you mind if I ask you something?"

"Ask away," she said, pulling out olive oil from a cupboard and dabbing it onto a paper towel.

"Did you and Ava talk? I mean, really talk about what happened the night her dad...disappeared?"

Ms. Goode didn't turn around as she responded, but she stopped fussing with preparing dinner. "Yes, Davey. I know what Ava believes about it."

"But you don't believe the same thing?"

Now Ms. Goode turned around and leaned back against the counter. "I know Ava is special, very special. But we don't know what really happened, do we? And more importantly, she hasn't wanted to talk about it since."

The librarian turned back to the stove and opened up a large drawer beneath it. She took out a large glass dish and set it on the counter, then rubbed the oily paper towel all over the inside.

Davey's cheeks grew hot. "So...that's it? You're just gonna let it go? Forget about everything that happened?"

Ms. Goode turned around again, her eyes sad. "Davey, I can never forget. You saw the Community Room. None of us can forget."

"But then why—"

"Because it's what she wants, Davey. And besides, the families around me have spent decades fighting against a belief in witchcraft. I would never encourage her to believe in her abilities, which she thinks are inherently bad. It's not healthy, and right now, she doesn't want to."

"But Ms. Goode, that curse came *true*. What about that?"

She nodded toward a table in the corner, surrounded by a panoramic view. "Let's sit down for a minute."

Davey took a seat opposite the window, Ms. Goode with her back to it.

"Davey, we're imposing our interpretation of the curse if we say it came true; who knows what Sarah Goode really meant. And are we saying she was a real witch after all, capable of making a curse come true? I don't think so. The Mathers did all of that work." She pushed her hair over one shoulder. "More importantly, though, I'm trying to give Ava what she wants. For the first time in her life." She gazed at Davey with a grave expression. "And she doesn't want to talk about it."

Davey tore his eyes from the view and slumped in his chair a bit. Ava always wanted to be cured, and then...well, maybe she was trying to be her own cure. And Ms. Goode was helping.

"I know," he mumbled, staring at the shiny wooden table top. "But Ms. Goode, I don't know if you know Ava like I do."

"Davey, I don't know if any of us truly know Ava."

That made Davey fall silent.

Davey sensed that was as far as he could push Ms. Goode, but he couldn't help himself. "What about her dad? What about what happened to him? Ava wouldn't make up something like that."

Ms. Goode stared out the window. "Davey, we can believe lots of things when we're traumatized."

Davey tried one last thing. "Ava said you think something happened when she was born. That it somehow made the Mathers stop trying to hurt your Community."

Ms. Goode continued to face the window. "I think the Mathers believed Ava was evidence that the curse was playing out—as demonstrated by what they named her. And that fear somehow...changed everything. For the better, as it turns out, for the Community."

Then she stood up and smiled. "Don't you need to call your mother?" She returned to the stove and started pulling out cooking utensils from drawers.

Davey studied the mountains, staring at the snow-covered peaks. He imagined flying above them, skimming treetops, then zooming upward to race an eagle.

He wanted to be happy for Ava. A swirl of words and images flew around in his head.

The look on Johnny's face when he saw Davey flashed in his mind.

The scary drawings of all the people on Ava's walls.

Her father's voice: *"She insisted on being called Evil...a broken child..."*

Then Ava's:

"... I thought I should warn you. I'm bad luck."

"I'm not good for you, Davey."

Davey rubbed his eyes, tried to shut out those thoughts.

He really wanted to be happy for Ava.

CHAPTER 24—EVIL

E vil smoothed the brownish-red sweater—*henna*, Aunt Julia called it—and admired her new flared pants. She opened her closet and looked for her flats with pointy toes. Real girl-shoes. They weren't exactly comfortable, but she loved the way they looked. When she couldn't find them, she closed the closet and turned around. The toes poked out from under the bed, and she bent down to retrieve them.

Her boxes of drawings, stuffed under her bed, briefly came into view. Evil stared for a moment, her smile fading, then grabbed the shoes and slipped them on. She bit her lip, then kneeled down again, diving far under her bed to slide out the closest box. She pulled apart the cardboard pieces and examined the statues of Ms. Goode and Davey resting on top of the drawings. Evil clutched the statues and whispered to them:

"Don't ever leave me."

She swiftly placed the figures back in the box, closed it up, and shoved it under her bed with her feet. Exhaling as she stood, she smoothed her clothes again. Footsteps in the hall drew her attention, and she pressed her ear to the door. Three different voices.

A man said, *"Julia knows what she's doing."*

"She's a child," a woman added.

"She's a Mather!" another woman hissed.

It had to be members of the Community. They were the only ones who lived here. The excuses her Aunt Julia made for why she hadn't met any of the Community yet, why Evil ate with her aunt privately in the kitchen instead of with the others, flitted around in her head. The dirty looks she got from a girl just a few years older than her who lived down the hall. Aunt Julia believed Evil was not just good but a gift. A mysterious gift to the Community.

But not everyone agrees with Aunt Julia...

The same voice of the woman who had said Evil was a Mather drifted under her door, as if she'd paused there, wanting Evil to hear her.

"She is rotten."

Evil's lips trembled and her eyes brimmed with tears. She gritted her teeth, but the trembling increased. She clenched her hands and raised them, stared in panic as her fingers flexed and clenched, fists turning into claws. She dropped to her knees and crawled toward the free-standing mirror where her backpack sat. Her backpack with her sketch pad in it.

"No," she whispered as she neared her backpack.

"No!" she growled and forced herself to stop. She wrapped her arms around her legs and buried her head in her knees as she rocked back and forth.

"I won't," she whispered, her voice muffled by her knees. "I won't draw, I won't hurt anyone! I won't!"

As she balled her hands into fists again, pain radiated from the middle of her back and blood seeped from beneath her nails. Small red drops dotted the floor. Evil gasped in horror at her bloody fingers and palms, but then something in the mirror made her raise her eyes. She gazed upward and grew cold and silent.

Her father stood there in his robes, touching his crest with one hand. As she raised her arm to point at him, his arm raised to point at her. His mouth opened, but his voice came out of her mouth.

"Evil," she said out loud, in her father's deep tone. "You cannot fool me. You're not even fooling yourself. We know who you really are."

She scrambled to her feet, and this time his motions didn't mimic hers. Her lower lip quivered as she glared at him.

"At least," she said to him in her own scratchy, quivering voice, "I know who I'm not."

Evil raised her bloody hands above her head and pressed them against the mirror. As the blood trickled from her fingers, the Reverend's image blurred and rippled until she stared through thin red bars into her own gray-blue eyes framed by bone-pale skin and scarlet tongues of hair.

Don't miss out!

Visit the website below and you can sign up to receive emails whenever Wendra Colleen publishes a new book. There's no charge and no obligation.

https://books2read.com/r/B-A-GUROB-JXIVD

BOOKS 2 READ

Connecting independent readers to independent writers.

About the Author

Wendra Colleen's motto is "Embrace your weirdness." Her dark and humorous short stories, screenplays, and novels show how unique, unusual, and unconventional individuals transform adversity into empowerment. Funky facts include that she has a PhD in experimental psychology and deployed to the Iraq War as a civilian, all of which was a breeze compared to learning how to embrace her unique, unusual, and unconventional qualities in high school. Want to learn more about Wendra's work, how to be a writer, or how to be empowered? Check out www.wendracolleen.com

Read more at www.wendracolleen.com.

www.ingramcontent.com/pod-product-compliance
Lightning Source LLC
Chambersburg PA
CBHW030312180626
46810CB00003B/1038